Roscoe Turner

From Plows to Planes

Roscoe Turner

From Plows to Planes

Boots Hensel

Kimber Court
PRESS

Roscoe Turner: From Plows to Planes by Boots Hensel

Copyright © 2020 by Carol "Boots" Hensel

ISBN: 978-0-9891822-2-5 (softcover)
ISBN: 978-0-9891822-3-2 (ebook)
Library of Congress Control Number: 2020911183

Published by Kimber Court Press
Panama City, FL 32401 USA

Kimber Court
PRESS

Photographs reprinted with permission from the American Heritage Center, University of Wyoming.

Book Design by Sun Editing & Book Design, suneditwrite.com

Printed and bound in the USA

Dedication

To Daddy, Grandpop, Lynwood, Bryce, James and Larry, the men in my life who with much effort shaped me into the woman I am today.

To my grandson, Ean, who often flies by the seat of his pants, and keeps his wings level for smooth landings.

To my granddaughter, Alayna, who has Roscoe Turner's "I'm not a quitter" attitude that I admire.

To my daughter Kimberly, who has made me a proud Mama and Nana.

Contents

Author's Note

ROSCOE TURNER: FROM PLOWS TO PLANES, dramatizes the life of flamboyant pilot Roscoe Turner, from his early days on the family farm to racing airplanes with his pet lion, Gilmore. Yes, he kept a real lion who accompanied him in the cockpit during his many flights. When he performed his stunts—maneuvering his planes in dives, death defying rolls and spins with heart stopping stalls—he proved beyond any doubt that taking risks excited him. Spellbound, audiences watched him walk on airplane wings and hang beneath them holding onto only a single guy-wire.

John Glenn, Jr., astronaut and senator from Ohio wrote in his autobiography, *John Glenn: A Memoir*, that at sixteen years old he watched Roscoe Turner fly at the Eighth Thompson Trophy Race. He and his father sat in the nosebleed section of the bleachers, which gave John a birds-eye view of Roscoe taking long strides toward his plane and climbing into the cockpit. All the planes lined up and waited for the signal to start the race. When the horn sounded, the men took to the air. The first pilot to cross the finish line after flying ten laps around pylons won. It was a tight race with Roscoe in the lead when one pilot flew close to his tail. In a skilled maneuver, Roscoe pulled his plane ahead leaving the other pilot in a swirl of exhaust smoke. John cheered Roscoe on and witnessed him win his second Thompson Trophy Race. Earning the nickname "The American Speed King," Roscoe flew speeds up to two-hundred and eighty miles an hour. "I can't believe anyone flies that fast," John said. "Someday I'll fly just like Roscoe Turner." His future unknown, John could not realize that one day he would be the first American astronaut to orbit the earth three times.

Roscoe Turner challenged the capabilities of flight with his raw courage, racing airplanes at speeds of over five-hundred miles an hour from the East Coast to the West Coast, and from the United States to Europe. His flying kept a glimmer of interest alive in aviation when very little public or governmental interest existed. Flying fast and far gave him opportunities to test the limits of aviation technology making airplanes fly higher, safer, better and farther. These advances impacted the outcome of World War II and became the foundation for supersonic and space flight.

Roscoe believed in the future of aviation and encouraged present generations to remember their forefathers, who by exploring flight advanced aviation and kept the United States above everyone else in the aeronautical sciences.

In writing the facts of Roscoe's life as fiction, rather than non-fiction, my desire is to engage the imagination of the reader. The main events in the book really happened. Roscoe's thoughts, actions, conversations, and interactions leading up to and surrounding these major events are as I imagine they might have been. In all, I hope I captured the innovative and pioneering spirit of Roscoe Turner, the master showman.

CHAPTER 1
The Need for Speed

"**W**hoa," Roscoe hollered at the mules when he heard the wail of the train. He looked up from the furrowed rows of plowed red clay while the train zoomed by the boundary of his family's farm in Corinth, Mississippi. The horn whistled when he waved at the engineer.

Roscoe had never met the engineer, but he thought of him as his friend since he tooted his whistle whenever Roscoe waved at him. Each time the train passed, he had the same thought, "I wish I was on the train. It must be fun going that fast."

"More fun than walking behind you two mules looking at your backsides all day," Roscoe said. With a shake of the reins that hung around his broad shoulders, and a giddy-up, he moved down the rows again. "Yes, sir, I want to be a train engineer when I grow up."

After he plowed the fields, Father came to see how he was doing. "You did a good job. You've helped me with the farm since you were old enough to toddle around. Now you're almost as tall as I am. I know that I can count on you doing your best. This field is proof of it."

"Thank you, Father. I know I'm growing. At the end of the school day, we race to see who gets out the door first. With my long legs, I always win. The kids call me granddaddy long legs, but I don't care, since I'm the winner. I'm going to start my chores around the barn now."

"That's good, son."

He mucked the stalls, slopped the pigs, and waited as long as possible to gather the fresh eggs. More often than not, Joe, the ornery rooster, surprised him out of nowhere making a beeline for his head, spurs fully extended. He always ducked, but sometimes Joe caught him and scratched the daylights out of his scalp. Despite Roscoe's thick hair and hat, Joe could still put a hurt on his head.

That is the meanest rooster this side of the Mississippi River. I'll take pig smell over Joe's chicken stink any day. I'll bolt through the chicken coop as fast as I can and maybe I'll catch him off guard.

He looked around the coop. There was no sign of Joe. Roscoe readied himself and in-a-flash reached under the sitting hens, grabbed the eggs, and cradled them in his hat. Then he raced out before Joe even had his feathers ruffled. He stepped onto the weathered back porch with the eggs and opened the screen door. The smell of his mother's fresh baked oatmeal cookies made his mouth water.

"Hi, Mother, here are the eggs." With one hand, he handed her the eggs and with his other hand, he grabbed several cookies. He stuffed one in his mouth and the others in his pocket.

She took the warm eggs and smiled. "I'm glad you like my cookies, son, but leave some for your brothers."

With only a quick wave, Roscoe headed out the door again, kicking up dust as he ran. On his way to the woods, he passed the open window and heard her say, "That boy is always in a hurry."

He slogged barefoot through swift creeks, plucked the last of the wild blackberries and popped the juicy fruit in his mouth. Once in a while he'd catch unsuspecting green spotted bullfrogs, but was careful picking them up, since they often peed on him! He had learned to hold them at arm's length and carefully place them back on the creek bank. He loved climbing the mighty elm trees and hanging out in the crook of the limbs. The leaves had turned a brilliant gold, a sign summer was coming to an end. Summer never lasted long enough. Soon he would be walking through these same woods with his brother to the one-room schoolhouse to start another school year.

ROSCOE TURNER ON THE LEFT WITH HIS BROTHER ABE PLOWING THE FIELDS OF THEIR FAMILY FARM.

CHAPTER 2

The Kite Disaster

Mr. Moreland stood at the front of the class in the one-room Glover County Schoolhouse to welcome his returning students. He began the day's lessons by reading the major historical events from The Daily Corinthian Newspaper. Roscoe paid particular attention to the article about the eight-year anniversary celebration of the Wright brothers' invention of the flying machine in 1903. His imagination went wild. *I wonder if I can fly like the Wright brothers? I bet if I build a kite large enough to carry me, I can fly too!*

On Saturday, Roscoe gathered thick twine, large sticks, a pot of glue, and old rags. Piece by piece, he made a kite frame. He wrapped the sticks and twine together and he glued the stretched rags from one stick to the other. When he finished the body of the kite, he tore smaller pieces of rags for the tail. After a couple hours, he had a three feet wide and six feet long kite big enough to carry him. Now how was he going to get it to fly? *What if I use one of the mules to pull me fast enough to get the kite in the air?*

He led Bessie, the fastest mule, from the field and attached one end of a long rope to her bridle. The other end he tied around his waist. He needed a good run from her today. With one hand he held the kite, and with his other hand, he tossed pebbles at Bessie's rump. She paid him no mind and grazed on the grass.

"Stubborn old mule." Roscoe tossed a few more pebbles at her bottom and yelled, "giddy-up," but she didn't budge. Not willing to give up, he thought of another plan. *I can jump off the barn roof and get enough wind under the kite to give lift and keep me in the air.*

Holding his kite, he climbed onto the creaky barn roof and carefully stepped to the edge.

He bent his knees and counted—"three, two, one," —and took a giant leap. For a second, he soared high in the air, but then, he plummeted straight to the ground, landing in a crumpled heap. He lay there for a few seconds catching his breath. Except for a couple skinned knees, he was okay. His kite survived the crash too..He picked himself up and carried his kite back to the barn. On the way, he saw Father running toward him followed by his brother Abe. Father's lips pinched together and his brow furrowed as he glared directly at Roscoe.

Uh oh, I'm in big trouble. Roscoe had seen that look before and it wasn't good.

"Roscoe, what were you thinking? You could have broken your neck!"

"I wanted to fly and I thought the kite was a good idea."

"You are always up to some adventure, but this was a hair-brained idea for sure. Never jump off that roof again! Don't you realize that as the oldest you have to set a good example for your brothers?"

"I promise I won't do that again, Father."

CHAPTER 3
Graduation

On Monday, just as school let out, Mr. Moreland pulled Roscoe aside. "Roscoe, you are the oldest in my class. I congratulate you for sticking with school for ten years. Most of my students quit after eight years. I think you've learned all I can teach you. It's time for you to graduate."

Roscoe wanted to jump for joy, but remembering he was still in the schoolhouse, he just smiled at Mr. Moreland.

"Bring your parents with you to watch me sign your diploma, first thing tomorrow morning," Mr. Moreland added, as he shook Roscoe's hand.

"Thank you very much. I can't wait to tell them."

Roscoe spied Abe, his younger brother, stuck at the back of the line that wound around the room. *He'll come soon enough; there is no time to wait for him today.*

Once outside, he whooped it up and did a jig. He ran most of the way home. When he reached the dirt road leading to the farmhouse, he yelled at the top of his lungs. "Mother, Father, I'm graduating."

Mother dropped her broom and Father ran in from the field, not sure what the commotion was about. "Mr. Moreland is signing my diploma tomorrow and he wants you both to be there."

"That's wonderful news," Father said.

"We are proud of you Roscoe, you are the first Turner to graduate," Mother chimed in.

Thunderstorms and rain kept Roscoe awake most of the night. It seemed he had just fallen asleep when he heard Joe's crowing, announcing the first light of day. He stumbled out of bed and dressed. Father was already sitting at the table when Roscoe walked into the kitchen. Mother was busy at the wood-burning stove making hot cakes and ham to celebrate the big occasion.

"Good morning," Father said. Mother turned from the stove and filled Roscoe's plate with the steaming hot food. "I'm sorry I won't be able to go with you this morning. Your brother, Cass, woke up with a fever and I can't leave. Abe can go with you and Father."

Roscoe's disappointment shows on his face, but he understands. After eating, Roscoe, Father and Abe, dressed in their Sunday best. Roscoe helped Abe with his tie and made sure he had his good shoes on. Abe hated wearing shoes and it wouldn't surprise Roscoe if he tried to go barefoot.

Standing at the door to leave, Mother approved how they all looked. Then she reminded Father not to forget the item in his pants pocket. He nodded, and she sent them on their way.

The overnight rains had turned the dry dirt road into such a muddy quagmire that Roscoe, Abe and Father had to maneuver around the puddles. Abe, three years younger, was Roscoe's constant shadow and walked beside him. Roscoe chuckled to think how muddy they would be if Father wasn't with them. When they arrived at the schoolhouse, Father made them knock mud from their shoes before they walked into the classroom.

"Hello, Roscoe and Mr. Turner, come right in. Abe, you can take your regular seat."

Mr. Moreland walked to his desk, picked up Roscoe's diploma and turned to the class where all the children sat at their desks. "Today, Roscoe has completed the requirements for high school graduation. May his accomplishments inspire each of you." He shook Roscoe's hand and gave him the signed diploma. "Congratulations young man, you have been a good student and I wish you the best."

Roscoe took the rolled-up piece of paper and glanced at his father's beaming face. The last time he had seen him smile that big was when they harvested a record corn crop last year.

Abe gave Roscoe a salute and Roscoe saluted back.

They said their "thank yous" and "goodbyes," and walked out the door leaving Abe to finish the school day. Standing on the schoolhouse porch, Father pulled a small brown-paper-wrapped box tied with string out of his pants pocket. He handed it to Roscoe and said, "I am happy for you and I want you to have this. It belonged to my father and now it's yours."

Roscoe untied the string, tore off the paper and opened the box. Laying on a swatch of mother's quilt, was a beautiful gold pocket watch.

"Oh Father, this is magnificent. I've never had anything this nice. Knowing this was your father's and now it's mine, means so much to me. I will treasure it always." He tucked the gift away in his pants pocket and they left for home.

CHAPTER 4
The Long Walk Home

Roscoe stared at his diploma, gripping it tightly. Father smiled and said, "You know son, with that diploma you have a good future ahead of you."

Roscoe held his breath and waited for what he thought Father would say next. He expected him to react poorly when he told him of his plans.

Father started, "I want you to—," but before he finished his sentence, Roscoe blurted out,

"Father, I don't want to stay on the farm. I don't want to be a farmer."

"That's exactly how I feel too. I'd like you to stay close enough to help me on occasion, but not all the time. I've always hoped your life to be easier than mine. I want you to go to Corinth Commercial College and become a business man, maybe even work in the bank."

Roscoe stopped dead in his tracks. Did he hear what he thought he heard Father say? Numbness overcame him and he didn't know what to say next. The unexpected words stung. Now he knew Father wouldn't be pleased about what he wanted to do. He collected his thoughts and looked straight into Father's eyes and said, "I don't want to go to commercial college either. I want to be a train engineer."

Father didn't seem to hear as he continued in a determined voice. "Roscoe, I took you into town with me to the bank many times so that you could see the dignified, smartly dressed bankers. People in the community respect them and they work inside every day. If you go to commercial college, you can work with them. I don't mind farming; it is good, honest work. But it is hard and backbreaking. I want better for you. I spoke with Corinth Commercial College and here's the list of courses you will take. I expect you to go and that's that."

Roscoe took the list, read it and hung his head. He gazed at the muddy road and tried to blink back tears. His heart was heavy. *I don't want to be a banker cooped up inside and doing the same things day after day: that's not for me. I want to feel the steam from the train boiler and smell the coal, wood and oil from the engines. Speeding down the tracks is my dream.*

They were quiet and when they reached the fork in the road, they took the way home. The other road circled back into town. Roscoe would rather have taken that one to avoid saying any more to Father, but he couldn't bring himself to walk away. Along the way, they dodged large mud puddles and ruts in the road. Just as they sidestepped a squishy rut, two speeding mud splattered race cars, with large red numbers on their doors, roared past them. The giant wheels with skinny black tires slid around the corner and splashed mud everywhere. Flying clumps of brown wet clay dripped from Father's hat. He yelled and shook his fists at the drivers, but they were long gone on their way back to town. Roscoe hadn't noticed the mud on his clothes. He was too fascinated by the race cars and the smell of engine oil. He stared at them until they were only specks in his vision.

A new dream entered Roscoe's mind. *Cars and trains go fast. Can I be a race car driver and a train engineer?*

CHAPTER 5
Corinth Commercial College

On Monday morning Roscoe pulled on his neatly pressed pants and shirt which immediately made him itch. "I don't belong in these clothes," he said to his reflection in the dresser mirror. "This isn't me. No matter how many business classes I take, I will never be a banker."

He turned from the mirror and with heavy footsteps left the room and headed to the kitchen. Father sat at the table with his ham, biscuits, and red-eye gravy. "Good morning, son."

Roscoe nodded, but didn't say a word. After a few moments of heavy silence, Father continued. "I know a business career is not what you want now, but in time you will understand I'm right."

Roscoe didn't respond. He knew if he said anything about how he felt, Father would roll his eyes, clench his jaw and give him an icy stare. So he ate his breakfast without speaking, cleared his plate, and left for classes.

He arrived at the classroom and settled into a seat near the open window where the curtains billowed from the gentle breeze. He liked being close to the windows. If a car drove past, he'd have a clear view of it. Even though Roscoe's family didn't own a car, he knew how to drive. Ben, the town mechanic, taught him last year. He loved hanging out at the repair garage on summer afternoons. Sometimes Ben even let him help, although mostly he just watched. A few more students shuffled in and Roscoe heard the low rumble of their voices while they quickly found their seats. Suddenly, the room fell silent and all eyes turned to a short, stocky man dressed in a three piece suit, and wire-rimmed glasses perched on the end of his nose. He entered the stage and with his powerful voice demanded their attention.

"Hello students, I'm Professor Simmons and I will be teaching bookkeeping, typewriting, shorthand, penmanship and commercial law. These are subjects you will use in your career."

I won't be using any of those subjects when I drive trains or race cars, but I will study them for Father.

I won't guarantee I'll ever work in a bank though. After an hour lecture, the professor dismissed them. Roscoe gathered his belongings and began his trek home. Thoughts swirled in his head. *I want to please Father and finish commercial college, but I never want to be a businessman. What am I going to do?*

Father rushed in from the fields when he saw Roscoe walking up the road. He caught up to him and asked, "How was your first day? Do you like your professor?"

Roscoe tried to sound enthusiastic when he told him about his day, but all he wanted was to change out of his scratchy clothes and get into his overalls. Father was relentless, peppering him with questions. He suddenly understood why Father was eager for him to go to commercial college. He really wanted to be a businessman, but never had the chance.

Roscoe decided to make the best of college for his father's sake. *Will he ever understand I have to follow my own dreams, not his?*

CHAPTER 6

The Rear Axle Mix-Up

One Friday, six months after starting commercial college, Roscoe walked down Fillmore Street to see if anything was happening in town. He paused at the large open metal doors of the familiar automobile repair shop, surprised to see a "Help Wanted" sign in the window. He looked inside for Ben. He spotted him in the back corner scratching his balding head as he stared at the disassembled car parts scattered on the floor all around him.

Roscoe called from the front as he walked across the grease-stained cement floor. He couldn't help but think of all the times he'd hung around as a kid watching Ben work his mechanic magic and bugging him with questions. Ben taught him everything he knew about cars.

"Hello, Ben, I saw your help wanted sign and I'd like to apply for the job."

"Hi, Roscoe, aren't you going to business college? Why do you want to work here?"

"I never wanted to be a businessman. Business college is my father's dream, not mine. I'd really like to work on cars instead."

Ben smiled, making the curls at the end of his thin mustache twitch. "Once you get your hands on car engines, you're hooked. Remember the Everett-Metzger-Flanders I taught you how to drive last summer? There's one over there with a stripped axle. Tell you what, if you put the rear axle back on I'll hire you."

"That's super, Ben. I'll put on a pair of coveralls." He watched Ben rummage through file drawers, tossing and rifling through each one like a squirrel digging for acorns. "I found it, the diagram of the gear assembly, follow it and you shouldn't have any trouble. Let me know when you're finished with the car."

Roscoe rolled up his sleeves and studied the E.M.F. diagram. After a couple hours of scraped knuckles and smashed fingers, he had the rear axle back on. Certain it looked exactly like the diagram, he called Ben for approval.

"Looks good Roscoe, but the test will be seeing how she runs." Roscoe jumped into the driver's seat and grabbed the steering wheel. Ben pushed from the rear bumper until they had the car on the road. Then Ben gave him the signal to start the car. Roscoe turned the ignition and Ben gave the car a crank. The engine hummed. He shifted into forward gear and pressed the gas pedal while Ben stood by the garage doors to watch. As soon as his foot pressed the gas, what happened next is not what he expected. The car lunged backwards! What's happening?

He turned his head in time to see Ben scramble for cover behind the garage wall. Shocked and confused, Roscoe forgot to step on the brakes. When the car came close to hitting the building, he heard Ben holler, "For goodness sakes, Roscoe, stomp on the brakes!"

Roscoe snapped out of his shock and slammed on the brakes. The car came to a screeching halt within a cat's whisker of crashing into the wall. For a minute he sat there bewildered at what had happened. He hardly noticed Ben come over to assess the situation until he spoke.

"It's okay, Roscoe, looks like you have three gears going in reverse and only one going forward. You've got the axle on backwards. I'll help you get it on right. You've got the job."

Roscoe beamed. "Thank you, Ben. When I drove in the wrong direction, I thought you'd never hire me. I'm surprised and extremely grateful."

"I hired you, Roscoe, because of your love of engines. I can teach you what you lack in mechanical knowledge, but I can't teach the emotional connection you have. I could see it in your eyes that you wanted this job more than anything. That was important to me. I'll see you Monday morning."

"See you, Ben. I'm excited to tell my parents I have the job!"

CHAPTER 7
Telling Father

Father confronted Roscoe the minute he stepped into the kitchen. "Why are you so late? Where did you get that smudge on your face? What happened?"

Roscoe pulled a rag out of his back pocket and rubbed the grease off as he flopped in a chair. "Um, well, you know today was the best day I've had since beginning commercial college."

"Really, Roscoe?"

"After classes today, I went downtown and noticed a help wanted sign at Ben's garage. I asked him for the job. He had me put a rear axle back on one of the cars and told me if I got it back on, he'd hire me. Well, I did with his help. He wants me to start work on Monday.

Father, I need to go out on my own and experience things for myself."

There was an awkward silence. Father looked down at the table, shook his head and spoke firmly. "Roscoe, I understand your spirit of adventure, but you have a good opportunity to be a businessman and I hate to see you throw that away."

Roscoe's stomach was in knots, but he sat quietly thinking of what to say next.

"Father, I don't like that you and I can't agree on this, but you don't understand what this means to me. I was happy in the garage and I'm determined to work there."

"Do what you must, but if you fail, don't come to me with your sad story."

"I will never fail, I'm not a quitter. I'll show you I can amount to something." He stormed out of the kitchen and out to the barn to do his evening chores. *On Monday morning I'll see Professor Simmons and tell him I won't be in class anymore.*

Roscoe whistled every morning as he headed to the garage. He didn't understand why Father couldn't see how happy working there made him. One day after he'd worked there almost a year, he arrived to see Ben bubbling over with excitement.

"Hi Roscoe, today is a special day. We will be working on the black car in the back. It's a Model T Ford, first made in 1908 and quite rare. In fact, in the last three years this is the only one I've seen. I can't wait to get into her engine. Let's get started."

They worked for hours on the car, and when they finally came out from under the hood, they had so much grease covering their faces that all they could see of each other was the whites of their eyes! They immediately bent over belly laughing. When Ben could stop laughing long enough, he said, "I hope I have enough rags to get all this grease off. Let's clean up. We'll start in the morning where we left off."

Roscoe laughed so hard tears ran down his cheeks. "See you tomorrow."

CHAPTER 8

The Test Drive

"**L**isten to that engine purr. I think we're ready for a good test drive, but it's getting pretty late. How would you like to drive the Model T home tonight? You can show your father the very car you worked on."

"Wow, Ben, that's great. I can't wait to drive it home."

Roscoe beamed as he waved to Ben. He headed down the bumpy road home, dodging ruts the dried red clay made to avoid getting dirt on the car. When he turned onto his road, he tooted the horn all the way until he reached the farmhouse. He saw Mother's eyes widen as she stood in the front of the farmhouse cradling William in her arms. Father came out, a confused look on his grim face. The rest of the family came running out too, first Abe, then Cass and Robert. But before any of his brothers reached the car, Father called out, "Roscoe, what in the world are you doing with that car?"

"Ben let me drive it home to show you. I've been working on it with him and he thought you'd like to look at the Model T."

In a firm voice, Father responded, "Son, if you keep messing around with things that go pop and are full of grease, you won't be worth a plumb nickel."

Once that was said, he and Mother walked into the house, calling the other two boys to follow them. This wasn't the reaction Roscoe expected. He sat in the car getting his thoughts together before he went inside. *I wanted Father to be proud of me and maybe even change his mind about me working on cars.* Roscoe now knew that he and Father would never agree about his future. He had decided for himself what he wanted to do in life. *I'm sixteen now and as much as I love working in the garage, do I want to be Ben's assistant forever?*

Roscoe always had a hankering to see places other than Corinth. At the last family reunion, his Aunt Mollie had said he was welcome to visit her at her boarding house in Memphis anytime. There were more cars in the big city, maybe even race cars. *That's what I'll do. I'll telegraph her first thing in the morning.*

The next morning, Roscoe cranked the Model T himself on the first try. The engine sputtered, then revved up and settled into its familiar rattle. It made him proud to know he'd helped to fix the car. He enjoyed the drive into town, thinking that this might be the last time he'd get to drive such a wonderful car. When he arrived at the garage, he spotted Ben standing in the doorway. "Good morning, young man. Well, how did she run? I bet your father was surprised when he saw you driving that nice car."

"The car runs perfectly, and—well—Father was surprised, but not in a good way. I enjoy working with you, Ben, but Father and I haven't been agreeing on me being here. I hate to go home at night 'cause I know he will fuss about me not going to commercial college."

Ben let out a long sigh and said, "I'm sorry about your father's disapproval."

"My aunt lives in Memphis and since it's a bigger town, there will probably be opportunities to find work there. I want to send her a telegram this morning asking if I can come stay with her."

CHAPTER 9
Leaving

R oscoe walked to the brick glass front Western Union telegraph office and stepped inside. He saw Mr. Spencer wearing his green visor and tapping out a dot and dash message, making clicking noises across thc wire.

"I'll be with you in a minute, Roscoe." When he finished, he asked, "What can I do for you?"

"I want to send a telegram asking my Aunt Mollie if I can stay with her."

"That's easy enough, I'll get that right out."

"Thanks, Mr. Spencer, how much do I owe you?"

"Thirty cents should cover it. I'll let you know when I get an answer back."

Roscoe paid the thirty cents and headed back to work. Then he dug right in to help Ben, putting in a full day. Just before closing time, Mr. Spencer's delivery boy found Roscoe in the back of the garage cleaning things up.

"Your Aunt Mollie's telegram came."

Ben gave the boy a nickel, as Roscoe tore open the envelope. A broad smile spread across his face as he read it.

"Whoopee! She says I can come right away and gives me instructions on how to find the boarding house."

"Looks like you're going to the big city of Memphis."

"Thanks, Ben, I'm going to miss you."

Roscoe wanted to give his friend a hug, but thought that would be too childish, so he just shook his hand before they went their separate ways.

In the morning Roscoe woke while it was still dark outside and stuffed what few clothes he owned into a flour sack. He quietly closed his bedroom door for the last time and tiptoed to his parent's bedroom. He lightly tapped on their door and picked at a string on the sack while he waited. The door creaked open and Father stood in front of him with a blank stare.

"Morning, Father, I came to tell you and Mother that I'm leaving home and moving to Memphis. I sent a telegram to Aunt Mollie asking permission to stay with her and she said it was alright. I'm catching the train to Memphis. I may be just a teenager, but I know the things I love to do, and banking isn't one of them. I don't want to argue with you anymore."

By this time, Mother heard the conversation and shuffled to the doorway. She looked as if she was about to cry, which dampened Roscoe's excitement a little.

While Roscoe talked, Father nodded and when he stopped talking, Father said, "I know it hasn't been easy, but what I've done and said is what I believed to be for your own good. I hope one day you will find this to be true. We wish you the best."

Roscoe thought at last they finally agreed on something. As he turned to leave, Mother called after him, "Take some leftover biscuits and an apple for the trip. Take care of yourself."

"Thank you, Mother, I will."

He walked to the kitchen on his way out and grabbed a couple biscuits from the plate and an apple, placing them in his sack. A bit of sadness hit him as he closed the door. He was going to miss Mother and his brothers, but he felt differently about his father. He couldn't wait to get away and prove his worth. *Someday I'll make him proud of me.*

CHAPTER 10

The Train Ride to Memphis

Roscoe arrived at the train station to see people dressed in their finest clothing carrying their fancy leather satchels. He wound his way through all the hustle and bustle to the ticket counter. He read the chalkboard that told him how much the fare would be to Memphis and then he reached into his pocket to pull out his money. He placed a wrinkled five-dollar bill on the counter and told the clerk he was going to Memphis.

"That will be four dollars and fifty cents, here's your ticket and your fifty cents change."

Roscoe took his ticket and found an empty bench where he could watch the trains approach. He unwrapped his apple and took one quick bite. Then he noticed a black dot down the tracks coming closer and closer as the rumbling chug-a-chug-a-chug grew louder. He jumped to his feet and shouted to no one in particular. "Hooray, here she comes." A few people chuckled at his enthusiasm, but he didn't care. His first train ride was something to shout about.

The platform conductor called, "All aboard to Memphis." Roscoe quickly stashed the rest of the apple in his sack and rushed to where the conductor stood at the bottom of the steps. He climbed aboard and sat on the nearest empty seat. More passengers boarded taking seats all around him. As soon as the seats were full, the train pulled away from the station. I can't believe I'm riding a train instead of just looking at one from far away.

His heart raced so fast with excitement that he could hardly sit still. *So, this is what the inside of a train looks like.* When he was a young boy and watched from the hill on the family farm, he could see the heads of the passengers, but he never could have imagined the interior.

Sitting in one of the high-backed seats was a man reading a newspaper. Across from him, a lady with a fancy hat adorning her head was applying lipstick. In another row, a man slept in his seat with a handkerchief over his face that moved with his every breath. His wife read a *Saturday Evening Post* magazine and occasionally glanced out of the large viewing window.

Roscoe loved the feel of going fast down the tracks. He had closed his eyes to just soak in the motion when the train conductor tapped him on his shoulder. "Do you have your ticket?"

Roscoe passed his ticket over. As he watched the conductor punch a hole in it, he said, "You know when I was a kid, all I wanted to do was drive a fast train. I loved trains, still do."

"Looks like you're riding all the way to Memphis. It will take us some time to get there. Do you want to meet the engineer?"

Roscoe smiled as wide as the Mississippi.

"By your expression, I think that is a yes. Follow me and I'll take you up to the cab." The ticket conductor introduced him to the engineer and left.

"Hello, have a seat behind me. I've got to keep my eyes on the tracks and gauges, so I won't be saying much."

Roscoe rubbed his eyes and coughed a little. The gritty dust from the coal bin was throat-choking and eye-stinging, but that was okay with him. He watched the fire-man shovel black coals into the red hot glowing fire-box. Sweat left streaks down the man's dust ridden face while he worked non-stop to satisfy the hungry box. Roscoe took his eyes from the fire-man and glanced back at the engineer.

"I used to stand on the hill over there waving at the trains and the engineers waved back at me. My Father always knew where to find me when he wanted me for chores."

"That was you? I've run this line for many years and always waved back at a young man on that very hill. I'm glad to know it was you. Welcome aboard."

At first, Roscoe watched every move the engineer made as he continually checked his gauges, making adjustments when needed. Eventually his eyes drifted to the window. Cows grazed in their fields and deer bravely leaped across the train tracks hurrying to the other side. Row upon row of neatly planted turnip greens peeked out of the ground. For miles and miles brilliant gold and red trees announced the change of season. He was so enthralled with the fast ride that he hadn't noticed the time. Before long they pulled into the Memphis station. He wanted to stay on the train, but Aunt Mollie was waiting.

Just before they reached the depot, the engineer turned to look at him. "Wanna blow the whistle?"

"I sure do." Roscoe reached up and tugged on the cord the engineer indicated. The whistle blew so loud it made his head throb, but that sound was music to his ears.

When the train came to a full stop, he thanked the engineer, picked up his sack and stepped down onto the wooden platform. Straight ahead was a directional sign that pointed the way to Aunt Mollie's Boarding House and he followed it.

CHAPTER 11
A New Beginning

Roscoe stepped from the train station into the bustling streets of Memphis. He dodged several townspeople scurrying around with their shopping goods. He marveled at the cars that zoomed by beeping their horns. As he walked past the open door of the barbershop, he got a familiar whiff of talcum powder. He couldn't believe there were so many people and shops. *I will definitely be able to find work in such a big city.*

Ahead Roscoe saw Mollie's Boarding House sign and his aunt waiting on the front porch. Smiling, he gave a big wave. She rushed down the steps and immediately flung her arms around his lanky body. Since he stood half a foot taller, he had to bend down to receive her bear hug.

"Roscoe, I'm glad you're here. I've been keeping an eye out for you all morning." She put her arm around his waist and led him into the house. "Let's go to your room. I made sure you'd have one with a front window view of downtown, where if you're so inclined," she said with a wink, "you'll be able to watch the comings and goings around here. The kitchen's downstairs toward the back and the washroom is at the end of the hall. I've got dinner cooking, so I'll leave you alone to settle in."

"Thanks, Aunt Mollie, for letting me stay here."

She smiled and closed the door.

He glanced around at the neatly made single bed with a patchwork quilt covering the mattress. The bed was arranged against one wall and an armoire stood in the corner. A lightbulb with a string attached to pull the light on and off hung from the ceiling, and one wicker chair next to the bed made up the rest of the sparsely furnished room. He took his clothes from the flour sack, laid them in the armoire, then ventured downstairs.

Aunt Mollie stood at the wood-burning stove stirring a large pot. She turned to him when she heard his footsteps. "Pull out a chair and sit a spell, tell me all about the family. How long will I have the pleasure of your company?"

"Aunt Mollie, I want to stay here as long as you let me. I can't live at the farm anymore. Father and I argue often. I want to find a job and live here in Memphis."

"Why do you argue with him?"

"I want to work in a garage and he wants me to be a banker working in a stuffy suit all day. I know he thinks it's best for me, but he won't listen to what I want."

"You know when your father and I were kids, he could be a little stubborn once he had his heart set on something. I think you have some of that stubbornness in you too."

"I guess I do, but I at least tried to please him. He doesn't want to give in any."

"I tell you what, after supper, we'll take my car for a tour around town. I'll show you a couple places that I know may need help."

After they caught up on the news, Aunt Mollie called the boarders down for supper. They trickled in and took their places around the table.

"This is my nephew from Corinth. He's looking for a job in a car repair shop. If any of you men hear of anything, let him know."

Each one introduced himself and shared his experiences looking for work. Roscoe took it all in. After supper, Roscoe helped Aunt Mollie tidy up the kitchen. Then she picked up her purse and motioned for him to follow her out the back door. As soon as he stepped onto the back porch, Roscoe spied the automobile. "Is that your car, Aunt Mollie?"

"It sure is."

"I can't believe it. This is an Everitt-Metzger-Flanders car. I learned how to drive on one just like it."

"In that case, Roscoe, why don't you take a seat behind the wheel. You can chauffeur me around town."

"That is great. Anytime you need to go somewhere, I'll be happy to drive you."

"Sounds like a good plan. I'll take you up on that offer. Now let's start her up and head to town."

CHAPTER 12
Job Hunting

Over and over Roscoe heard, "We don't hire teenagers." It looked like he wasn't going to be able to find a job as a mechanic's assistant. At the last garage he stopped in, the owner told him that he'd heard the Wholesale Grocery Cooperative down the street was looking for a shipping clerk. "I'm sure I can do that."

Roscoe hurried out the door and walked down the block to the store. A brass bell tinkled announcing his arrival when he pushed open the door. A man with deep-set blue-green eyes and wispy brown hair that hung over his glasses gave him a good long look. "Hello, I'm Clarence Saunders," the man said in a deep voice. "I'm the owner, is there something I can help you with?"

"I'm Roscoe Turner, Mollie Bailey's nephew from Corinth. I'm looking for a job. I heard you need a shipping clerk."

"Yes, I do. Can you keep track of the trucks coming in with their deliveries? The pay is seven dollars a week. Think you can do the work?"

"I'm sure I can."

"Can you start right now?"

"Yes, sir. Thank you very much, sir."

Mr. Saunders showed Roscoe how to record each delivery truck as it pulled into the wooden loading dock. It wasn't hard, and over the next few weeks, Roscoe began to get a little bored with it. He did enjoy meeting the truck drivers and hearing of their adventures on the road.

One ice-truck driver, Tom, liked him and offered to take him along on his ice deliveries when Roscoe had a day off. They rode together so often that Roscoe knew the routes by heart. A few times, Tom even let Roscoe drive the powerful truck. One day, Tom told Roscoe he was quitting for another job.

"You'd make a good driver, you already know the routes. Why don't you ride with me tomorrow afternoon? I'll take you to the ice house for an interview."

Roscoe really wanted the job and agreed to Tom's plan.

The next afternoon, after he swept the floors and turned the closed sign on the door, Roscoe peeked through the shade and saw Tom waiting. He shut the door for the night and hopped into Tom's ice truck. While they drove down the winding road to the Wilson Power and Light Company Ice Plant, Tom gave Roscoe advice on what to say to help him get the job.

"Make sure you act like you know what you're doin'. Whatever you do, don't mention you're only sixteen. You're tall and unless he asks, there's no need to say anything. Tell him you already know the routes and that you've worked in a garage in Corinth. He'll be impressed with that."

"I will, Tom."

They pulled into the parking area and Roscoe strolled in with his shoulders erect. "Hello, anybody here?" He heard a shuffling noise letting him know someone was coming.

"I'm over here." A broad-shouldered man stopped before he reached Roscoe. Probably because he didn't want to maneuver around different stages of melting ice. "You must be Roscoe. Tom told me you would be applying for the job. Follow me. Be careful, dodge the slippery ice."

His office was full of papers with no particular order, or at least that's what Roscoe thought. The boss, as he was known, propped his arms on the small desk and leaned forward. "So, tell me why you think you should have the job."

"I'm way ahead of anyone else who applies for the job 'cause I already know Tom's routes. I'd also be able to keep your truck in good running order since I've worked on engines in a garage in Corinth."

The boss's bushy eyebrows raised and he chuckled when he heard that. "Sounds like I'd be foolish not to hire you, young man. Now go tell Tom you're hired."

Roscoe jumped off the crate he was sitting on and shook boss's hand. "You won't be sorry you hired me. I'll be the best driver you've ever had."

CHAPTER 13
Trucks, Cadillacs, Packards, and More

Each morning before beginning his deliveries, Roscoe maneuvered large three-hundred-pound blocks of ice, by sawing them into manageable sizes. Then he'd pick them up with ice tongs and lift them into the truck for deliveries. Although he enjoyed this work, he still longed to drive something that went faster than the truck.

One day when he took the truck to get the oil changed, he noticed an older gentleman with grey hair at the temples. He turned to the mechanic who was working on his car. "Who's that?"

"That's Mr. Robert R. Price, the garage owner and president of the Southern Motor Car Company. He owns the only Cadillac dealership in the city."

Impressed, Roscoe walked over and introduced himself. "Mr. Price, the Cadillac is beautiful. What I wouldn't give to work on an engine like this!"

"Oh, are you a mechanic?"

"I worked as a mechanic's assistant back in Corinth. I love engines and anything that goes fast and burns fuel."

"Sounds like I need to have you working with me. You're hired!"

Roscoe couldn't believe his luck. At first he assisted the mechanics, and once in a while they'd give him odd jobs around the garage to earn more money. One day, as he handed the mechanic a wrench, he looked up to see a Cadillac roll in with a chauffeur behind the wheel and a passenger in the back seat. Roscoe gave a long whistle, followed by, "Great day in the mornin', what a beautiful car."

The mechanic slid out from under the car to see what the excitement was about. "That's Mr. Hill, he's president of Union and Planters Bank and Trust. That Cadillac he's riding in, is the first one sold in Memphis. Once a month, he brings it into the shop to get it serviced. He's a nice, down-to-earth man, and even though he lives in that mansion on Union Street, you'd never know he's wealthy."

"I don't know how nice or wealthy he is, but he sure has a great car."

Mr. Hill climbed down from the back seat and tipped his hat to those standing around him. His fair-skin contrasted to his dark suit and top hat. Roscoe thought him the stateliest man he had ever seen.

He looked directly at Roscoe, probably because he was the only man Mr. Hill didn't know. "Are you Roscoe?"

"Yes, sir, that's me."

"Mr. Price told me how good you are with automobiles. I'm looking for a part-time chauffeur. My present driver can't work seven days a week without a day off, so I'm asking around for someone who can help me out. Mr. Price recommended you."

"I'd like to, Mr. Hill, but I don't want anything to happen to my job here."

"Oh, don't worry. Mr. Price and I are good friends and he's assured me he will work out a schedule, so as not to interfere with anything here. What do you say?"

"If it's okay with Mr. Price, then it's okay with me. I'll be happy to drive this beauty of a Cadillac."

"Good, then it's a deal."

CHAPTER 14
Memphis Fairgrounds

One evening after Roscoe drove Mr. Hill home from the bank, he walked back to the boarding house, enjoying the quiet night. Then all of a sudden, he heard a loud roar and looked up. A massive military airplane flew over the fairgrounds, spreading the bright colored flares from its wingtips across the evening sky. He kept his eyes on the magnificent display as he ran to the fairgrounds.

He arrived at the same time the plane landed and joined the already assembled crowd. As soon as the propellers stopped spinning everyone ran to greet the pilot. He couldn't believe his eyes, when out of the cockpit, a dainty woman appeared. Her glossy brown curls fell below her shoulders. How could she fly like that? She shook some hands, then as quickly as she had landed, she disappeared in the throng of fans. Listening to some of the crowd, Roscoe learned the woman's name was Katherine Stinson, an aviatrix who earned her flying license when she was twenty-one years old. *She's only three years older than me. If she can fly, I bet I can too.*

This was the beginning of his love of flight. From that moment on, his aspiration was to take a skyward direction. For the next few months, he talked to anyone who would listen about his new dream, but most of those listening just shook their heads as if to say, "Flying, who would want to do a crazy thing like that?"

Driving Mr. Hill, and working at the garage, kept Roscoe busy. When he wasn't working, he enjoyed the conversations with the other men at the boarding house and settled into a routine.

Twice a day for three years, he had strolled past the Memphis Fairgrounds going to and from work. He still remembered the first time he saw an airplane there. This evening, as he neared the area, his eyes caught sight of airplanes lined up wing to wing in the vast open fairgrounds. Each wing gleamed in the sunlight. He glanced from plane to plane taking it all in. He stopped at the gate and read the sign, Come One and All! See Army Pilots and Their Single-Seat Biplanes! The pilots were gathered by their planes dressed in their jackets, breeches, and shiny brown leather boots that came just below their knees. They slapped each other's backs, having a good time chuckling at each other's jokes. A small crowd began to form.

Roscoe didn't have to be anywhere in particular, so he sprinted over to the pilots. When he reached them, he tilted his head to one side and listened to their stories of executing spins and falls from the sky. Each nose dive and death spiral maneuver was an evasive tactic in case enemy planes dogged them. In spite of imagining at any minute their planes could explode into piles of smoking rubble, they kept their cool and made it home to tell of their near-death encounters.

Their electrifying tales made the hairs on Roscoe's arms stand up. *Pilots must have nerves of steel to fly like that. I wonder if I have what it takes to be a pilot? Planes go fast and I love going fast.* More questions swirled in his mind. How did they become pilots? Did any of them crash? He wanted to ask, but he remained quiet and spellbound, not wanting to interrupt a single story.

He pulled out the pocket-watch his father had given him and checked the time. He knew if he didn't leave, he would miss dinner and Aunt Mollie would worry. He didn't want that to happen, so he turned away, glancing back, wishing he could stay. *Someday I'll fly!*

CHAPTER 15
The Big Disappointment

Bubbling over with excitement, Roscoe made it home in time for dinner. He told Aunt Molllie and her boarders about the army pilots and their magnificent airplanes. "I want to fly so bad, I can taste it. You can bet your bottom dollar that one day I'm going to be sitting in the cockpit of an airplane."

The men sitting at the table listened and smiled. His enthusiasm was contagious and pretty soon they all were talking with him about how he might accomplish his goal. None of them had an exact strategy, but they supported him.

On Monday when he arrived at the garage, he retold almost every word the pilots spoke. The mechanics listened, but no one had any ideas how he could fulfill his dream.

Mr. Rich, overheard his story and said, "Roscoe, you are strong-willed and whatever you set your mind to, you will do. One day your time will come and when that happens, I will be right by your side."

"Thank you, Mr. Rich. I'm living part of my dream. You know how I love engines and going fast. I just figure airplanes are the next step to going even faster."

"You've been with me for three years now, and I always knew there was going to be something else down the road for you. I believe you should always be looking toward your next adventure and I'm sure you have many of them ahead of you."

The rest of the week, Roscoe worked alongside the mechanics and kept thinking about how exciting it had been to listen to the pilots' stories. He couldn't get that day out of his head, but he didn't really want to forget.

One Saturday morning, Roscoe moseyed down to the kitchen, hungry for breakfast. Most of the boarders were around the table drinking coffee and talking about their week. As he sat down, one of the men said, "Mornin' Roscoe, I heard the army is now training young men for the air service. I thought you'd like to know. You lovin' airplanes and all."

Roscoe jumped up and almost spilled his coffee. "That's it, that's how I can fly! See you later."

He flew out the door like the house was on fire, with not even a biscuit in his pocket, but he heard one of the men say, "I bet he gets to fly yet."

When he reached the door of the Army Air Service office, he stopped to catch his breath after the six-block run. Then he walked into the small room filled with clerks clicking away on their typewriters. The clerk nearest the door looked up, "You need something?"

"I'm here to apply for flight training."

"Have a seat and fill out this questionnaire, when you're finished bring it back to me."

Roscoe found the closest empty spot where there was a pencil and began answering the questions. The first one asked his address and age. He gave the boarding house address and put twenty-one in the age blank. Next, they wanted to know if he had a college degree. He wrote that he had attended Corinth Commercial College, but that he hadn't graduated. The rest of the questionnaire asked him to list any health or vision problems. He answered everything and then handed the questionnaire back to the clerk.

"All right, let's see what you have here. Hmm, you're old enough and in good health. You work in a garage, and you've had experience driving an ice truck. Wait a minute, there is one problem." Roscoe held his breath. "You don't have a college degree. The air corps only trains college graduates for flight school."

"Oh no," Roscoe said, staring at the clerk as if trying to understand what he just heard.

"Sorry, son, but that's the rule."

With slumped shoulders, he left and slowly walked home. He made his way to the kitchen where some of the men were still talking at the table. They looked up at him, and one asked, "How did it go?"

"Not too good. They won't take me in flight training 'cause I don't have a college degree. I know there are rules, but one day I'm still gonna fly. I'm not sure how, but I will. I'm a Turner and we don't quit."

Later that evening everyone gathered around the radio in the parlor to hear President Wilson talk about if the United States entered the war, in Europe, they could help France overcome aggressive Germany, and that the world would be a safer place. He asked Congress to declare war against Germany, and they approved his request. When the president finished his speech, the radio announcer said, "Folks, mark this as a history making day, April 6, 1917."

CHAPTER 16
The Army

L ike many young men of that time, Roscoe wanted to help his country fight the war. On Monday, April 16, 1917, he walked into the Army Recruiting Office in downtown Memphis and stepped up to the counter. "Hello sir, I'm here to enlist in the Army."

"Take a seat and Sgt. Maxwell will help you."

The sergeant waved Roscoe over to the empty seat and began the enlistment process by asking Roscoe questions to fill out the paperwork.

"What is your occupation?"

"Right now, I work as a junior mechanic and driver, but before that, I drove an ice truck. In Corinth, I was a mechanic's assistant."

"Perfect, you will be a good match for assignment to the ambulance corps where you'll drive and maintain the motor pool ambulances. Report for your physical and basic training at Fort Riley, Kansas, one month from today."

"Yes, Sergeant." As Roscoe closed the door, he knew his life was about to change in a big way.

He hurried home, hollering as he entered, "I'm in the Army. I've been assigned to Kansas for basic training."

Aunt Mollie ran from the kitchen with her apron strings dangling and her potato peeler in one hand. She met Roscoe in the hallway and wrapped her arms around him. "Roscoe, I'm so proud and happy for you, although sad you will be leaving."

"I'll miss you too, especially your cooking, but the Army needs me."

Roscoe arrived at Fort Riley in the evening on May 16th. After getting his bunk assignment, he stowed away his few belongings. Before he could introduce himself to the other men in his platoon, a thin blonde-haired man strode into the barracks and called them to attention.

ROSCOE TURNER IN HIS MILITARY UNIFORM.

"I'm Sgt. Riley, your platoon leader. Tomorrow you will report for your physical and fitness tests at zero seven hundred hours. If you pass, you will be issued uniforms and gear. On Friday, you will report for basic training. I will see you then." After he gave the instructions, he sharply turned and left the room.

Roscoe introduced himself to the other men in his unit and they chatted until the bugle played taps. Exhausted from the journey and excitement, he fell right to sleep, despite the hardness of the unfamiliar bunk.

At sunrise, the reveille bugle sounded, waking everyone up. It didn't bother Roscoe since he was used to old Joe, that ornery rooster, waking him up with his loud crowing. He dressed and followed the other men to the mess hall. The induction station was next door, so after eating, he and the other recruits stood in line waiting to be measured, weighed, and checked from their heads to their toes and all the areas in between. Each man was issued a uniform and gear then told to report at zero seven hundred hours for training. Roscoe gathered his gear and went back to his barracks where he organized his belongings and neatly placed them in his footlocker at the end of his bunk. After a busy day, he looked forward to a good night's sleep.

The next morning, Roscoe was awake and ready before the bugle played. From early morning until sunset, he and his buddies learned basic drill, military discipline, physical fitness, how to use a weapon and mental preparation for war. The training continued for eight weeks. Then he received new orders to report to Camp Dodge, Iowa, for advanced training for overseas duty in France.

Two days after receiving his orders, he boarded a train heading for his next duty station. Listening to the trains' wheels against the tracks, he thought back to his first train ride. That seemed so long ago.

CHAPTER 17
The New Assignment

Roscoe knew the drill of finding a bunk and squaring away his gear when he arrived at Camp Dodge. He sailed through the start of advanced training, and did so well that his superiors promoted him to sergeant. All the while though, he kept remembering the Army airplanes at the fairgrounds. *If the Army would give me a chance, I'd show them I can be a great pilot.*

One morning, he heard news that the U.S. Army Balloon Corps Cadet Program was accepting applications. *Balloons aren't the same as airplanes, but they fly.* He walked the dirt path to his company headquarters to fill out the necessary paperwork. Then he waited and waited to hear if he was accepted. One month passed. Then two, and still no news. *How long does it take?*

Finally, after a three-month agonizing wait, an envelope addressed to Sgt. First Class Roscoe Turner arrived. He ripped it open and pulled out the folded paper and read, "Congratulations Sgt. Turner. You are ordered to report on February 1, 1918, to the Balloon Pilot/Observer Cadet Training Program, at Camp John Wise Aerostation, San Antonio, Texas." He stood in the middle of the barracks and hollered, "At last, I'm going to fly!" A couple of the men raised him up on their shoulders and carried him around the barracks. He lost count of how many times they hoisted him in the air to celebrate the good news.

I have two weeks to get ready. That will give me enough time to visit Aunt Mollie and get some home cookin'.

He sent a telegraph letting her know he was heading her way for a visit before his next assignment. Two days later, he walked in the front door and yelled as loud as he could, "Aunt Mollie, I'm here and guess what, I'm going to fly!"

She bolted from the kitchen, while boarders stepped out from their rooms and hung over the bannister wondering what the commotion was all about. "I've been accepted to the U.S. Army Balloon Pilot/Observer Corps Program. I leave in two weeks for training."

"That's fantastic, Roscoe. I always knew you'd find u way to fly."

Lt. John Hall stood at the front of the classroom at Camp Wise, wearing a starched khaki uniform with the air corps insignia patch proudly displayed above his left shirt pocket. He began, "On your desks you will see booklets with diagrams of balloons you will eventually fly. Study them well. In the next four months you will learn map reading, basket repair, how to generate hydrogen, parachute rigging, balloon operating procedures and the science of weather."

For two months, Roscoe and the others sat on hard desk seats and poured over balloon diagrams until one day, they finally heard Lt. Hall say, "Meet me at the training field tomorrow at zero eight hundred hours for your first balloon flight lesson."

The next morning, Roscoe marched to the training field to join the other cadets standing in formation. From where he stood, he counted nine grey balloons tethered around the field, each one blending in well with the overcast skies. The cadets came to attention when Lt. Hall marched toward them.

Thoughts raced around Roscoe's head. *I know I want to fly, but in a wicker basket with a flame shooting out of the center? Have I completely lost my mind?*

CHAPTER 18
Flying Balloons

L t. Hall stood before the gathered group of cadets, "Men, today you will fly your own training balloons. Once you reach altitude, you will jump out of your baskets. The ground crew will take care of your balloons."

Did he just say we are going to jump out? Roscoe struggled to remain at attention, despite a desire to run.

Lt. Hall continued, "While flying over enemy territory, you are easy targets. If you are fired upon you have two choices. One is to parachute from your balloons and hope for a good landing. The other is to go down in flames with your basket. I'd say the second choice is not the best one."

Enemy fire? I'm not sure this is what I signed up for. Panic almost overtook him, until his sense of adventure kicked in. *This might be fun.*

"Now men, climb into the first basket you come to and strap on your parachutes. Once you are secure, open the hydrogen gas nozzle for lift off. When you reach gliding altitude, climb on the basket's edge and jump clear of your balloon. Count to ten, then and only then, pull your parachute ripcords. You will drift about twenty-five miles to the landing zone where ground crews will pick you up."

Roscoe and the other cadets found their assigned balloons and climbed in. He strapped on the parachute, then opened the gas nozzle on the balloon, and lifted off. He couldn't believe once he was in the air that he had to jump out of a perfectly good balloon. He chuckled when he remembered the time he jumped off the barn roof. *At least this time I have a parachute!*

The cool mist from a cloud formation blew across his face. He glanced over the edge of the basket and watched the ground crew scurry around like ants running from their hill. He kept watching the ground. Objects got smaller and smaller. *This is the highest I've ever been in my life.* His knees shook and his mouth was so dry he didn't have enough saliva to even spit in the wind. One by one, the other cadets jumped free from their balloons. He didn't want to be the last one out. *No one is going to call me a chicken!*

He balanced on the edge and started to count, one … two … and before he got to three, his foot slipped and he tumbled out. When he cleared his balloon, he counted to ten and pulled his ripcord. Uh-oh, nothing happened. The parachute was stuck! *Will this be my first and last jump?* As he wiggled the ripcord, the ground came closer and closer. All his muscles tensed. Just before he smashed into a million pieces, his canopy snapped open and jerked him back up. *Phew, that was close.* Now he could relax and glide toward the landing zone.

Then, out of nowhere, came a strong wind. It whipped through his parachute, driving him off course. *Oh no. I'm heading toward that telephone pole!* There was no stopping the collision. He stuck his legs straight out to brace himself for impact. A second later, he slammed right onto the top of the pole. He was caught and dangled high above the ground like a spider without its web. Surely the ground crew saw his parachute open, or did they? *How can they know I'm swinging from a telephone pole?* In spite of sharp shoulder pain, he felt for his three-point release snap. Then he pressed it. The snap didn't release. He wiggled and twisted, but was completely tangled in all the cords.

He hung there trying to figure out what he was going to do to get out of this pickle. *I'm really stuck. I can't even reach the top of the pole to untangle myself.* He began yelling, "Hello, anybody out there? I'm over here." He didn't know how long he had been yelling, but it was long enough that his throat was dry. Then he heard a voice. "Sgt. Turner? Sgt. Turner?"

He hollered at the voice. "I'm here, caught on a telephone pole."

When the crew member neared, he looked up to see Roscoe dangling. He broke out in a hearty laugh.

"This isn't funny, now help get me down."

The crew member climbed the telephone pole. Then he swung Roscoe so that when his legs came near the pole, he could wrap them around it. While Roscoe held on with his legs, the crew member took his handy Swiss Army knife and cut the knotted cords. Once Roscoe was free, he shimmied down the pole like a monkey. "I sure am glad you're here. How did you find me?"

"Each ground crew member had certain parachutes they were to watch. My job was to keep an eye on your parachute. I saw you drift off course. Then I calculated the wind direction and had a hunch where you'd be. I didn't expect you to be caught on a telephone pole though."

"Neither did I, but considering what might have happened, I'd say I'm a lucky fella."

"Let's get back to the field where the other cadets are waiting, Sergeant."

"Sounds good to me. Let's not mention I was tangled on a telephone pole. It will be our secret. If word gets out, I won't be able to live it down."

"My lips are sealed."

Roscoe planned on no one ever finding out. He was happy his first balloon flight was over. He had fallen out of the basket and lived to see another day.

After many successful balloon flights, he completed the aerial observer course. He was commissioned a second lieutenant, free balloon pilot in the Aviation Section, Signal Corps Reserve, on March 19, 1918.

CHAPTER 19

France

On June 14, 1918, Roscoe, along with other troops, took steamships across the Atlantic Ocean to join the men already stationed in France. A month later Roscoe stepped on solid ground after weeks of swaying back and forth on the ocean waves.

He and the other men climbed in trucks and tank convoys to ride to Pont-a-Mousson on the Moselle River. As soon as he arrived at the barracks, Roscoe unpacked his duffle bag, then hurried to the airfield to check out the balloons. He noticed several airplanes parked farther down the field. When he neared the closest airplane something appeared to move inside. He immediately stopped, stared at the object and didn't move a hair. He had been trained to be observant at all times and this odd movement made him on edge.

For a few moments he stayed frozen until the object stood up. When he saw it was a tall man with somewhat unruly hair, wearing olive colored coveralls, he relaxed. Roscoe called to him, "Howdy, I'm Lt. Roscoe Turner, stationed here with the balloon observation aviation section of the signal corps. I just arrived from the states and wanted to check around. Then I saw you moving around in the airplane."

"I'm Jefferson, I've been flying airplanes here for three months. Welcome."

"Any problems with your plane?"

"No mechanical problems. I'm checking her out from nose to tail though. This plane is new to us. She's powered by a liberty engine. Instead of using castor oil for lubrication, she uses water. That makes her less messy and much faster. I can reach one hundred and forty-three miles per hour in this girl."

"Wow, that's amazing. I'd love to see her engine. Do you mind if I look with you?"

"Not at all, come on up."

For the next hour, Roscoe and Jefferson bent over the engine checking every detail. They discovered both of them grew up on a farm and loved airplanes. After that, they hung out together as often as time permitted and developed a friendship. Pretty soon one wasn't seen without the other. They talked about home, airplanes, going fast, and whatever else was on their minds.

Roscoe had his twenty-second birthday three months after he arrived in France. He didn't realize Jefferson knew until his friend sent him a message, "Meet me at sixteen hundred hours in the hangar and don't tell a soul."

Roscoe wondered all day what Jefferson had planned. Exactly at the stroke of sixteen hundred hours, he went to meet his friend. There, in the pilot seat of his army airplane with the propeller spinning, Jefferson sat. He directed Roscoe to climb up. He hopped onto the wing and climbed in the open front cockpit. Jefferson tapped him on the shoulder and told him to put on his goggles and parachute. After Roscoe geared up, he watched Jefferson open the throttle. They were off, bumping down the runway.

When they reached the end, Jefferson pulled back on the control stick and up they went toward the clear blue sky. He reached altitude and leveled the wings. All of a sudden, he pushed the control stick forward and they immediately pitched downward. They were in a nose dive. As if going nose first toward the ground wasn't scary enough, suddenly the engine stalled, causing the plane to spiral out of control. Did Jefferson do that on purpose? Or were they really going to crash? Roscoe held onto the sides of the seat in a white-knuckled grip. His body stiffened, tense with fear. He was so scared he hardly noticed that Jefferson had re-started the engine and leveled the wings again. He heard Jefferson yell, "Roscoe, breathe, we're okay."

Roscoe's heart raced so much that he felt the pulse in his ears. He didn't want to show it, but his whole body was shaking. He released the grip on the seat with relief when he heard Jefferson shout, "I've gotta get this plane back before anyone knows she's missing."

They landed and taxied to the hangar. Once they came to a complete stop, both of them jumped from their cockpits. Jefferson glanced at Roscoe. "Are you alright? You look a little pale and weak in the knees."

"I'm fine now that I'm standing on the ground and not spinning like a top. I thought I was going to die."

Jefferson laughed and slapped him on the back. "Attaboy Roscoe. You have what it takes to be a pilot."

CHAPTER 20
First Flying Lesson

While Roscoe watched Jefferson tinker around the airplanes, he wondered how he could fly more often with him. He loved his balloon flights, but they didn't come close to flying as fast as the airplanes. Then an idea came to him. "Jefferson, I've been thinking. What if you take me with you as your observer? If I have a job, then neither of us will get into trouble."

"Great idea. Why don't you start now? I need to log in some flying hours and you can be my observer. I've been thinking, what would you say if I give you a few flying lessons?"

"Terrific! Teach me everything you know. Then I can execute death spirals like you."

"Whoa, hold on buddy. First, you have to learn about the airplane. For instance, you probably know the control stick moves the plane in all directions. But do you know that you have to use ailerons on the tip of the wings to bank the plane left or right? These are things I will show you. The stunts will come later after you've mastered the basics."

Roscoe smiled, then said. "I understand. Going fast is in my nature. I want to hurry through the basics to get to the fun stuff."

Jefferson climbed into the cockpit in the back and Roscoe slipped into the front observer seat. They strapped their parachutes to their backs and tied the leather pieces on their hats to secure the ear flaps. Roscoe gave a thumbs up and Jefferson rumbled down the runway gaining speed with every bump. At the end of the runway, Jefferson pulled up the nose and they were off.

The plane climbed into the white cottony clouds and when they leveled out, Roscoe looked down at the ordered rows of planted corn. The sight reminded him of his family's farm. He wished Father could see him now. Jefferson's hollering brought him out of his deep thoughts.

"Roscoe, concentrate on what I'm telling you. I'll repeat since you weren't paying attention the first time. Okay, here's your first lesson. To fly at a lower altitude, you push the control stick forward. If you want to go higher, you pull it back towards you. When you want to bank a left turn, you press your foot on the left rudder and with the left aileron up, the plane makes a roll to the left. If you want to go to the right, press your foot on the right rudder and position the right aileron up. Got that?"

Roscoe nodded.

Jefferson continued shouting over the engine. "Now, even more important is knowing what to do if your engine stalls and you go into a death spiral that you can't recover from. You must be familiar with your parachute. There is no time for hesitation."

"You don't need to worry about me and parachutes. Let's just say I'm very familiar with them from balloon flight school and leave it at that." Now was not the time to tell Jefferson about his telephone pole mishap.

After flying a little while longer, Jefferson tapped Roscoe on his shoulder motioning he was going back down. Roscoe hollered, "Okay." Soon they were on the landing strip, taxiing to the hangar. When the plane stopped, they took off their gear and hopped out of the airplane.

"That was great, Jefferson. I learned a lot today. When can we go again?"

"You're eager, aren't you? We'll keep at this as often as we can. Soon you'll know as much as me."

"That's what I'm hoping for. I've dreamed of flying ever since I saw my first plane in Memphis. I have never forgotten that feeling. I was eighteen then, now I'm twenty-two. I can't believe I have actually flown in a cockpit. It seems I've been waiting my whole life for this.

"One day you will fly on your own. I know it."

"I hope you're right. If that happens, I will be the happiest man on earth."

CHAPTER 21
In The Cockpit

Roscoe quickly climbed into the rear cockpit and studied the instrument panel while Jefferson grabbed the propeller blade. He'd grown quite comfortable in the pilot's seat over the last few weeks of flying lessons. The engine spit for a second and then roared. Jefferson hopped up on the wing and climbed into the front seat. Off they jostled down the runway.

When Roscoe reached the needed speed, he pulled back on the control stick, then up they went. Once they reached cruising altitude, he leveled the wings, but not for long. A big grin spread across his face while he thought of his next move. Eager to show

Jefferson what he had learned, he maneuvered the plane in big loops and several rolls. Jefferson gave him the thumbs up. Then came the last stunt. Not to be outdone by Jefferson, he aimed the nose downward putting the plane into a spin and stalled the engine. They were in a death spiral, heading straight for the ground! Jefferson, not trusting Roscoe's abilities yet, hollered back at Roscoe, "What are you doing? Pull her up! Pull her up now!"

Roscoe chuckled and hollered back, "Jefferson, breathe, we're okay." Jefferson cracked a smile remembering that he had done the very same thing to Roscoe months earlier.

After flying more flips and turns, the gas tank showed almost empty. Roscoe started his descent. When the wheels touched the ground, he taxied back to the hangar. They took off their goggles and hopped out as soon as the propeller stopped spinning. Jefferson looked at Roscoe, "You had me going for a minute. I thought, if we crash land and survive, how will I explain a smashed airplane to the commander?"

"I wasn't worried," Roscoe said, as he slapped Jefferson's back. "I had a good teacher. I remembered everything you taught me. Plus, I knew if I ran into trouble, I had you right there in the front cockpit."

"Well, you certainly don't lack confidence. I like that. When you fly solo, you will need it."

They walked a few steps in thoughtful silence, then Jefferson continued, "Have you thought about what you're going to do once you're out of the Army?"

Roscoe paused and scratched his head while he thought of an answer. "I have, and I don't know if there will be a job for me at home. I'm hoping I'll be able to continue flying. I don't want to give it up. I'm hooked. An airplane fuels my need for speed and excitement." He walked over to the plane and patted her side panel. "I can't imagine anything else I would love more than flying."

"Have you ever heard of barnstorming and wing-walking? A lot of former army pilots do that," Jefferson said.

"Isn't barnstorming simply flying in air shows? I've never heard of wing-walking. What's that?"

"Yes, barnstorming got its name from the air shows being at farms in towns that didn't have fairgrounds, but now it means travelling from town to town. Wing-walking is one of the stunts they do with a partner."

"You mean a guy gets out when the plane is in the air and actually walks on the wing? That sounds nuts, but I've got to see it!"

"Yes, we pilots are a unique breed. We're tough as nails and probably a little crazy. Who else in their right mind would purposely fly a plane into a death spiral or walk on a moving wing? Our mechanic is an experienced wing-walker. I'll get him to show you what he does."

Roscoe laughed. "I know my father would question my sanity. But, I'm in good company. There are two crazy guys standing here."

"You were born to fly, Roscoe."

"Thanks, Jefferson, for a great day. I'll never forget it."

They refueled and tidied up the hangar before they left for the day.

CHAPTER 22
Wing-Walking

The next morning, as promised, Jefferson found a willing wing-walking instructor, and introduced him. "Roscoe, this is Jim. He's our top mechanic and he'll show you the ropes."

"Nice to meet you, Jim. This is going to be exciting."

"Yep, maybe more excitement than you want."

"You haven't known me very long, but when you get to know me better, you'll see that the more daring, the better I like it."

"Well, I'm glad to have a chance to get out of the hangar. Let's get to it then."

Roscoe climbed behind the controls, with Jim in the front cockpit. Jefferson waved and they were off.

Roscoe felt his heart beating hard against his chest. His adrenalin flowed and it excited him. As soon as they were above the clouds, he watched while Jim stepped out on the wing holding onto a guide wire. Roscoe held his breath until Jim gained his balance and released the wire. He saw Jim struggle against the strong wind that made his pants flap like a bird taking flight. It seemed Jim only held on by putting all his weight into his legs and feet to secure his position.

Roscoe held the airplane steady, observed Jim in wonder and awe. *Do I dare learn to do that?* A mixture of fear and excitement rose at the possibilities ahead. After a few more demonstrations, they returned to the landing strip.

"That was amazing, Jim. You'll have to tell me your secrets."

"There's no secret. You have to concentrate on your balance. Focus on each foot placement. As you know, we don't have safety nets. We have no parachutes, they would be too bulky, and there are no safety wires. One slip of the foot and you'll be in a death spiral without a plane. I'm afraid that would not end well. I'll show you how I balance myself and you can take it from there."

"I'm ready to learn. You have my full attention."

For several months, with Jefferson at the control stick, Roscoe gained more confidence in his ability to walk on the wing of the airplane. He carefully calculated each step he made. At first he'd gingerly take baby steps across the wing. Then he'd hold his arms steady letting the wind blow past him. He'd stay there for about ten minutes before sliding his feet back to the cockpit. On one occasion, he and Jefferson had taken off on a clear afternoon for a practice run. Once the plane was level and steady, Roscoe climbed out and was determined he would stay even longer on the wing. Neither Jefferson nor Roscoe expected anything to go wrong, but in a matter of minutes a rain storm approached with high winds. Roscoe was caught. Rather than have the wind blow him off the wing, he crouched down on his hands and knees and crawled to the cockpit.

"That was a close call, Roscoe," Jefferson hollered above the thunder noise. "You could have been blown off. Glad you hunkered down and made it back."

"Me, too. I don't ever want that to happen again."

Jefferson and Roscoe trained often with him nearly falling off a couple of times, but he recovered without incident, much to his and Jefferson's relief.

CHAPTER 23

Barnstorming

After two months of sailing the ocean from France to the United States, Roscoe looked forward to seeing his family again. *I can't wait to tell them all about learning to fly.*

When he arrived at the farmhouse, his parents celebrated his return, expressing pride in his military service. His brothers gathered around to hear his tales of flying both in balloons and planes. For a brief time, Roscoe felt happy to be there. However, his happiness turned to disappointment when he told his parents he wanted to find a job flying. Father insisted he work in the bank. Mother agreed. Nothing had changed or would change their minds, so Roscoe caught the train for Memphis after only a short visit.

When he walked into the Memphis station, he noticed a middle-aged man who sported a long brown mustache that wiggled when he moved. The man took fliers from a pouch and tacked them up on a bulletin board. Curious, Roscoe strolled over to the wall and read: "The Memphis Aerial Company is hiring experienced pilots for barnstorming and wing-walking exhibitions across the country."

Roscoe couldn't believe his good fortune. He wasted no time introducing himself to the man. "Hello sir, I'm Lt. Roscoe Turner. I've just returned from the war. Officially I was a balloon pilot, but unofficially I flew airplanes like the best of them. I have nerves of steel and I can walk on wings and perform other daring stunts. I want to apply for the job."

"Hello, Lieutenant. I'm E.F. Young, the front man for Memphis Aerial Company. I travel ahead of the barnstormers to promote aerial shows and airplane rides. You say you know how to wing-walk?"

"Yep, I learned while I was in France."

"I'll put you in touch with Lt. Harry Runser, a former Army pilot, who performs the flying exhibitions. He will be the one to decide if you can join him."

Roscoe and Lt. Runser met a week later. After introductions and some questioning, Harry said,

"I need an experienced wing-walker. How about joining me?"

"Harry, you've got a partner."

Harry flew the plane while Roscoe was the alternate pilot, mechanic, wing-walker and general stunt man. They made a good team.

After three months of barnstorming, Roscoe became an expert at frightening anxious crowds with his wing-walking and falling from them. Of course, he knew he had a parachute, but those holding their breath below thought he was falling to his death until at the last minute his parachute opened.

Mr. Young booked an exhibition in Corinth, Mississippi, in front of Roscoe's hometown crowd. Roscoe and Harry planned a dramatic stunt with Roscoe falling from the wing. Then Harry would fly through one side of a house and out the other side. To set up the stunt, they built a flimsy house from the thinnest materials they could find. The house had to collapse on impact without destroying the airplane or Harry. The only sturdy supports were four brick columns where the walls were attached. Harry was to fly through the house in between the columns and exit on the other side, leaving the brick columns intact.

The day of the event arrived; a crowd formed, eager to see their home-boy. Ben closed the garage early.

Mr. Moreland, there to see his former student, yelled to Roscoe before they took off. "Be careful." Roscoe seeing him, gave him a sharp salute.

They took off with Harry at the controls and Roscoe in the front seat. Roscoe climbed onto the wing and balanced himself. Harry pushed the control stick forward making the plane descend toward the house. The crowd, unusually quiet, feared the worst. Roscoe readied himself to jump from the wing in plenty of time before Harry made impact into the fragile house.

Roscoe jumped scaring the onlookers. They hadn't seen his parachute. He landed on one of the side streets. Harry did not have the same good fortune. On impact, the planes' wings caught the brick columns and tore off. Roscoe ran the couple of blocks from where he parachuted to see Harry's precarious situation. Harry struggled to guide the plane to a safe landing without its' wings. The plane slid to a stop and Roscoe hurried to Harry.

"Are you okay? That was some landing!"

"I'm fine, but it looks like we won't be flying this plane for a while."

As they surveyed the damage, Ben came over to Roscoe and shook his hand. "I'm proud of your military service and your amazing exhibition. You're living your dream of speed."

"Thanks Ben. I wouldn't be here if you hadn't helped me years ago." Ben smiled and left Roscoe and Harry to figure out how they were going to fix the plane.

"After this mishap, I say we don't perform this stunt again," Harry said.

Roscoe agreed.

CHAPTER 24

On His Own

"You know, Harry, we've been performing our dare-devil stunts together for two years. I feel so confident about my flying ability, that I bought my own plane."

"Good for you, Roscoe. What did you get?"

"She's a beat-up Curtiss Jenny. I've been scouring around for surplus parts to repair her. Come take a look at her with me."

"I'd like that."

When they approached the Jenny, Harry let out a whistle. He took a moment and blinked a few times before he said, "She's a beaut, but you have your work cut out for you."

"Once I get all the parts, it won't take long to get her flying."

"If anyone can do it, it's you, Roscoe."

Roscoe worked long hours repairing the Jenny. After six months she was back together. He was ready for the test flight. He started her up. On the first try, her propellers whirred and the engine hummed. He pulled the throttle and sped up. Her wheels lifted off the ground and she was in the air.

While he soared among the clouds, he thought how much he enjoyed the feeling of control. *I wonder if I can do my own stunt flying? When I land I'll talk to Harry about it.*

After a problem free flight, he parked his plane and found Harry piddling around in the hangar.

"I'm glad you're still here. Now that I have my own plane, I'm thinking about doing stunts by myself. I'm ready to spread my own wings."

"I figured it would only be a short time before you struck out by yourself. I'm sure you'll be fine."

"Thanks Harry. I appreciate what you've done to train me."

Now it was time to fly home to Corinth to show the Jenny to his family. He sent a telegram letting his parents know their oldest son was returning. As soon as Roscoe approached the Corinth airfield, he saw Mother waving her handkerchief. He rocked his wings in an airplane wave back at her. As soon as his wheels touched down, she rushed toward him. Mother gave him a big hug, then said,

"I'm happy you're home, Roscoe."

"I'm glad to be home too. Where's Father?"

"He stayed at the farm. You know how he feels about you and airplanes."

"I know, Mother." Roscoe understood, but it bothered him. "I'm going to look for my own place."

"I heard of an apartment near the airfield." Mother grabbed her handbag. "Let's go look at it."

They walked a few blocks to the apartment building and found the landlord who gave them the key to the front door. When they walked in, Roscoe went to the bedroom while Mother poked around in the kitchen. They met in the living room and Mother asked, "Well, what do you think?"

"It's small but convenient to my airplane. Did the kitchen pass inspection?"

"There's a nice stove and small refrigerator which will suit you just fine."

"I'll take it then." Roscoe paid the first month rent and settled in.

From his new place, he traveled all over the country performing barnstorming events on his own. His daring airshows drew great crowds who watched him stride to his cockpit wearing his trademark robin's-egg blue coat trimmed in gold braid over his tan breeches. Newspapers wrote articles announcing his shows, which caused even more people to make their way to the fairgrounds or hired farmers' fields. Some spread blankets out for picnics. Others sat on their car hoods to watch his amazing roll overs, loops and spins. They expressed their awe of his skill when they paid for a short ride in his Jenny.

Roscoe took advantage of his fame, but after one year, realized there was little fortune to be had barnstorming. Most of the money he earned was spent buying gas and paying farmers to use their barns and fields. Maintaining his plane in tip-top condition also cut into the amount of money he made. Crowds dwindled and were nervous about paying for rides in his patched-up Jenny.

After two more years of strenuous use, his already old airplane started to wear down. "You've been a good plane, Jenny, but it's time for you to retire," he said as he patted her side.

He thought about other ways to use his flying skills. *Maybe I can compete in national and international races. I've got to get a better airplane if I want to win any races.*

Using his saved barnstorming money, he purchased a second airplane. It was a Sikorsky that flew much faster. He hoped the Sikorsky would be his ticket to racing success.

CHAPTER 25
California Bound

When Roscoe wasn't racing, he flew passengers from place to place. Living in the small town of Corinth meant less opportunities to pick up flying contracts, so he moved his base of operation to Atlanta, Georgia. He predicted that area would become a hub for commercial flight, and he wanted to be in the midst of it.

Although he now lived farther away, he visited his family at home whenever he could. On approach to the Corinth airfield, he always buzzed the farm, chuckling at how the chickens scattered. He had taken Mother and his siblings flying with him many times, but Father always refused the offer.

On a bright pleasant morning in 1927, Roscoe helped his mother settle into the co-pilot seat where she liked to ride. "Roscoe fly over our farm, but don't buzz the chickens. Your father will be fit to be tied if you do that again."

When they were over their farmhouse, Roscoe and Mother waved at the younger boys in the front yard playing ball. Midway between Corinth and their destination in New York, Roscoe landed to refuel. While the men gassed up his plane, he and Mother stayed in their seats. To pass the time, he began talking. "I have a new opportunity, Mother. A movie producer in Hollywood called me yesterday. He wants to rent my airplane for one of his movies. He may even need me to fly stunts in some of the scenes."

"That is exciting, Roscoe. What did you tell him?"

"I told him I'd think about it. I will have to move to California, where the movies are made. That means I won't be able to visit as often."

"I understand, Roscoe. Since you were a little boy you've had that wanderlust look in your eyes. You go where your heart and the next adventure leads you."

"Thank you, Mother. I'm glad you understand."

With the plane fueled, they set off into the blue sky again. Roscoe now had the answer for the Hollywood producer. He was going to take the offer and move to the big state of California.

A couple weeks later Roscoe landed at the Los Angeles Airport. His first stop was the movie company office. The producer offered to lease Roscoe's Sikorsky airplane for $11,000 making monthly payments for the entire time it took to complete the movie. On top of that, they would pay him gas money for his trip from the East Coast to California. Eager to have the job, he quickly read and signed the contract.

The producer converted Roscoe's Sikorsky airplane into a supposed replica of a German war plane to fit the theme of his war movie. It was their secret and the public wouldn't be told it really wasn't a German airplane. During the filming, Roscoe flew one hundred and twenty-two stunt flights, accruing many miles on the Sikorsky's engine.

One day, he wanted to take the plane for a maintenance check. The producer became furious. He did not want to postpone filming for one week while Roscoe took the plane for its check-up. He demanded Roscoe leave the plane. Roscoe then realized he had made a terrible mistake in signing that contract. It stated that once lease payments equaled the value of the plane, ownership reverted from Roscoe to the producer.

Upon discovering he no longer owned his plane, Roscoe drove off the movie set and never looked back. He stayed in California, but now he needed to find another airplane.

With money he had saved, he bought a fast Lockheed Vega and entered airplane races again. He loved racing. Being the first one to set a record for how fast or how far an airplane could go thrilled him. Even when he didn't win, he learned something valuable that helped him race better the next time. Could he make a bigger engine? Did the airplane's body rattle too much? Was the fuel consumption too great?

Most of his flights were testing grounds for building future models of airplanes. Little did he know that aeronautical engineers would study his improvements to design bigger, faster, and safer airplanes for generations to come. Each improvement Roscoe made increased the overall acceptance of airplane travel.

CHAPTER 26
Finding a Sponsor

Roscoe touched down in his Lockheed Vega after winning a stunning long-distance race from New York to Los Angeles. Throngs of people, including newspaper reporters and their photographers, waited for him as he climbed out of his open cockpit. He had won in record time, but it had been a long, grueling flight.

Once he saw all the admiring fans, his face lit up with a broad smile. He stopped to greet them. "Ladies and gentlemen, as much as I enjoy a good win after a long race, it is not only for fame and fortune that I fly. I want you to understand what I believe in my heart.

Airplanes are important for your future. They can improve our military strength and carry mail, goods, and people from one coast to the other, faster than any other mode of transportation."

Although Roscoe had won, he knew he needed an even better plane to stay ahead. There was always someone coming along trying to beat him with a faster airplane. Lockheed made a fast airplane, and he wanted the latest model.

In 1929 it was common for pilots to fly around the country advertising for major oil companies with their logos painted on the sides and tails of the planes. Roscoe kept his ears and eyes open for his own promotional opportunities. He hadn't seen anyone flying for Gilmore Oil Company. *If I can convince Gilmore Oil to hire me, then I can buy a faster airplane.*

All weekend, ideas came to mind on how to advertise for the future success of the oil company. Early on Monday morning, he picked up the phone and dialed Mr. Gilmore's number. He waited on the line a short time and heard a male voice on the other end.

"Hello, this is Earl Gilmore, who am I speaking with?"

"This is Roscoe Turner. I'm not certain you know me, but I have won several prestigious air races and have something to tell you that I believe will advance your business."

"Roscoe, how could I not know of you? I have been following your air speed records for some time and I know you are an accomplished pilot. What do you have in mind?"

"Recently I set the transcontinental speed record when I flew in a Lockheed Vega from New York to Los Angeles; it was an impressively fast airplane. There is a newer one I'd like to fly, and it's the Lockheed Air Express. With that airplane I know I will win more races and if you agree to sponsor me, I will advertise your company's logo on that very airplane."

ROSCOE TURNER IN FRONT OF HIS NEWLY DESIGNED AIRPLANE WITH THE GILMORE OIL COMPANY LOGO.

"Mr. Turner, with your flair for publicity and your flying skills, I can't refuse. Let's get to work."

"Thank you, Mr. Gilmore, you won't be disappointed. We will make a great team."

After Roscoe hung up, he got in his car and drove down the road. As he rode along, he thought of ways to advertise Gilmore Oil Company. He happened to look up ahead at a billboard; in bold colors was the big red Gilmore Lion Head Motor Oil logo. That's it, I need a real lion to fly with me. After all, the company mascot is a lion. I'm certain I'll get lots of publicity. Now he was on the look-out for a lion cub.

CHAPTER 27

Choosing Gilmore

With Roscoe's former connections in Hollywood, he heard about Goebel Lion Farm that bred and trained lions for the movies. He immediately gave them a call. At the other end of the telephone a voice said, "Hello, Goebel Lion Farm, Louis Goebel speaking."

"Hello, Mr. Goebel, my name is Roscoe Turner. I have an idea for a new business venture with Gilmore Oil Company. Their logo is a lion and having one fly with me while I advertise for them would draw attention. That publicity will be good for business. Do you have any cubs I can look at?"

"Well, it isn't everyday someone calls me with that request. It is an intriguing idea. Yes, I have a litter born three weeks ago that you can pick a cub from if you want. Come to my farm and see them for yourself."

"All right, see you tomorrow."

Roscoe spent the rest of the day preparing for the new family addition. He built a large enclosure in his backyard and explained to his dog, a fifty-pound black and brown spotted mutt named Contact, that soon he would have a playmate. He didn't mention that it was a lion cub. Roscoe hoped they would get along.

The next afternoon, he pulled into the driveway of Goebel's Lion Farm. Mr. Goebel showed him the three balls of yellow-gold fur. "Which one do you like?"

Roscoe looked down at the squirming cubs. One in particular was quite active and mewed the loudest, drowning out all the other cubs. "I want the wiggliest one making all that racket."

Mr. Goebel handed the energetic cub to Roscoe. It was all Roscoe could do to keep the cub from climbing out of his arms. Mr. Goebel agreed to let Roscoe pay him a small amount now and work out the rest owed by advertising the lion farm. They shook hands on the deal. Roscoe placed the cub in the crate in the backseat of his car and off they went back home.

"What am I going to call you little fella? I have to think of a good name for you. How about Goldie? No, that's not good enough. Maybe Leo? No, that name doesn't suit you either. I know, I'll call you Gilmore. It is a fitting name for the Gilmore Oil Company's mascot."

The rambunctious cub quickly became part of the Turner family. Gilmore and Contact became pals, much to Roscoe's relief. They chased each other all throughout the house, nearly knocking the furniture over. On one of their many chases, Roscoe watched as Gilmore, tired from all the running around, completely stopped and collapsed on the floor for a cat nap. Contact wasn't ready to stop the game and nipped the cub on his back legs trying to make him get up and keep playing. The mutt kept nipping and retreating until Gilmore swiped the annoying dog with one big slap of his huge paw across Contact's muzzle. The dog let out a loud yelp, as Gilmore sent him sprawling across the floor. He ran out of the room with his tail tucked. Gilmore got what he wanted and laid back down for his nap. Contact never disturbed Gilmore during nap time again.

CHAPTER 28

Gilmore's First Flight

The cub grew fast. When he was six months old, Roscoe decided it was time for his first airplane ride. "You can't be much of a copilot unless you like flying."

Roscoe hooked a leash to Gilmore's collar and led him to the airplane. He picked up the now sixty-pound cub and plopped him in the backseat cockpit. Gilmore sat with such a regal attitude that Roscoe had to laugh. "You're the king of the beasts alright."

After he had Gilmore situated, Roscoe hopped in the front seat. He set the flaps, started the engine, rumbled down the runway and off they went. The loud engine noise and the bumping motion scared Gilmore. All of a sudden, he wasn't so regal anymore. In one quick movement he clamped his big paws with his razor-sharp claws around Roscoe's neck, holding on as if his life depended on it. When Roscoe attempted to unclamp him, Gilmore dug in even deeper. The plane rocked while Roscoe struggled to unlatch the frightened cub.

After some coaxing, he managed to pull Gilmore's paws from his neck, then the cub latched onto Roscoe's seat. "It's okay, Gilmore, we'll land soon. You hold onto the seat and you'll be fine."

During the rest of the flight, Gilmore mewed almost as loud as any full-grown lion, or it seemed that loud. He didn't have his full roar yet, but his shrill noise made Roscoe wonder why he had chosen the noisiest cub of the litter. After flying a little longer, he figured Gilmore had had enough and landed. When the propeller stopped whirring, Roscoe climbed out onto the wing.

When Gilmore saw Roscoe stand up, he leaped into Roscoe's arms. "This was only your first flight, fella, you will feel better next time, Gilmore."

Roscoe was patient, doing the same flying routine with Gilmore, day after day. A couple months later, Gilmore had calmed down. Now his favorite thing to do was hide under the seat. One day, after many tries, Roscoe placed Gilmore in the copilot seat and took off. He pulled the control stick back and they began their climb. Gilmore didn't scramble under the seat, instead he sat still and actually fell asleep! No amount of jostling or engine noise woke him. Whatever the reason, Roscoe was happy he now had his copilot.

As Gilmore grew in weight and love of flying, Roscoe entered many races with him as his copilot. When Roscoe busied himself putting the planes through vigorous tests, checking their ability to tolerate high speeds and distances, Gilmore happily slept in the cockpit.

ROSCOE WITH GILMORE THE CUB SITTING IN THE GILMORE AIRPLANE.

ROSCOE HOLDING GILMORE WITH HIS CUSTOM-MADE PARACHUTE.

Gilmore on stand with Roscoe beside him.

The pair always attracted reporters and photographers who cheered when they saw Gilmore in the winning plane. Once after a big race, Roscoe taxied his plane to a complete stop, unhooked Gilmore, and let him off the plane. When the media crowd saw a now one-hundred-pound lion padding toward them at full speed, they all scattered, racing to a nearby hangar for shelter. Eager to meet everyone, the big lion didn't understand why the crowd was screaming and running away. He thought they were playing a game of chase!

Roscoe heard the ruckus and called Gilmore to his side. The big cat reluctantly obeyed and Roscoe got a good laugh. Eventually, the media crowd laughed too when they realized Gilmore had no intention of eating them.

CHAPTER 29
The Dynamic Duo

After a long non-racing flight from Los Angeles to New York, Roscoe and Gilmore landed with no fanfare.

"It's quiet, Gilmore. I know you love attention, but I'm sure you won't be disappointed once we get to the hotel. As hard as you're tugging on the leash, you must be ready to get there."

They walked a couple blocks, and then stood in front of the hotel. The doorman greeted them.

"Good afternoon, Mr. Roscoe and Gilmore. I see you're back with us again. Be prepared for excitement, we have a new desk clerk. None of us mentioned you were coming. So, we will have a little entertainment at his expense."

"I remember when they did the same thing to you, Milton. I thought you'd jump out of your skin the first time you saw Gilmore and me walking down the street toward you."

As Milton opened the door for them, he chuckled and said, "Yes, sir, that was a good one on me. Have a nice stay."

Roscoe and Gilmore moved toward the reception desk where the clerk was busy putting door keys in their cubbies. Roscoe tapped the silver bell sitting next to the registry. When the clerk turned around, he leaped back at the sight of Gilmore.

"Goodness gracious! That is a large animal. We don't allow any pets sir; much less a gigantic lion. You'll have to leave."

"Let me speak with your manager, please."

"Yes, sir," he said as he called his manager.

A man with a broad smile that almost made his eyes disappear came to the desk.

"Welcome back, Mr. Turner and Gilmore. I see you met our new desk clerk. He is a little shy of large animals, and extremely afraid of lions. He'll get used to Gilmore though. I'll get the ink pad for our usual paw registry signing."

Moments later, the manager carried a large ink pad made especially for Gilmore. He took Gilmore's paw, coated it with ink, then placed it on the registry taking up the entire page.

"Well done, Gilmore. Now I'll wipe that ink off and you can be on your way to your room."

After settling in, Roscoe's stomach growled. "I'm hungry, Gilmore, let's go to our favorite restaurant." When they arrived, all eyes turned as the maitre d' showed them to their table.

"Hello, Mr. Turner and Gilmore, I'll be right with you," the waiter said, holding his tray high so that Gilmore couldn't sniff what he carried.

"Don't worry about Gilmore grabbing the food today. I fed him before we left Los Angeles. He's not hungry, but I'm starving."

The waiter took Roscoe's order and in no time served his favorite roast beef and potatoes. When he finished eating, they left for a stroll down Fifth Avenue toward Central Park.

Everywhere the two went, they caused swarms of people to gather. After all, seeing a lion walk down the street would make anyone want to take another look. Not everyone was happy with the large mass of fur, muscle and roars. A few people screamed and ran away. Traffic all but stopped, a few cars barely missed colliding.

But the daring ones followed them, and some even asked to pet Gilmore. One brave boy came up to the lion and patted his head. Gilmore licked his face with his big raspy tongue. The boy giggled, "His tongue is scratchy like my kitten's."

Police officers on horseback rode toward them to control the crowd of onlookers. When Gilmore saw the horses, he wanted to play with them. He bolted from Roscoe's side and gave chase. Roscoe quickly followed, but couldn't help laughing at the sight of galloping horses, police officers clambering to stay atop their steeds, and a huge lion racing after them down Fifth Avenue.

After a frightening few minutes, Gilmore realized the horses were not in the mood to play and he gave up the chase. As soon as Gilmore stopped, the horses quit running away. The police officers caught their breath and regained their composure.

When Roscoe got closer to Gilmore, an angry police officer said, "I'm giving you a ticket for disturbing the peace."

Another police officer interrupted, "Don't you know, that's Roscoe Turner, the famous pilot and his flying lion?"

The first officer stared at Roscoe, clearly impressed. "I'm sorry Mr. Turner, I didn't recognize you. I was going to write you a citation, but instead, may I have your autograph?"

Roscoe laughed when the officer handed him his citation notebook. After signing his name, he glanced down at Gilmore. Then, winking at the officers, he said, "You know, boy, we're lucky you weren't hungry."

Roscoe and Gilmore continued their walk, while the officers followed at a safe distance.

ROSCOE TURNER AND GILMORE IN FRONT OF WARNER THEATRE ON WILSHIRE BOULEVARD IN LOS ANGELES.

CHAPTER 30

Gilmore Retires

C lear skies and cool weather made for a perfect airplane 1930 Derby race-day in Cleveland, Ohio. Gilmore lay in the front cockpit while Roscoe readied himself for the take-off signal. He took deep breaths, trying to calm his pre-race jitters. He heard a report that one hundred thousand people jammed into the overflowing grandstands waiting for the excitement to begin.

"I bet they're all here to see you, Gilmore, and look, you couldn't be bothered." He grinned as Gilmore yawned and gave him a lazy glance.

Nine fast air racers including Roscoe, lined up wing-tip to wing-tip. Fifty-foot-high pylons stretched across

Ohio's countryside marking the ten-mile course. The first one to arrive back at the start after flying the two-hundred-mile course would win. The signal sounded and all the planes' propellers roared on take-off.

The first to cross the starting line, Roscoe jumped into the lead. The sky was his. The airspeed indicator showed he was going three hundred miles per hour in every turn. The amount of force made his stomach feel like it was in his throat, but he couldn't slow down now. Planes flew close behind him. After passing several pylons, he pulled out the throttle to go faster, but nothing happened. The plane didn't accelerate. The engine sounded fine. What could be wrong? "We're in trouble, Gilmore, I can't go any faster."

Roscoe tried everything he could to keep ahead of the others, but with only one lap to go, the distance became greater and he fell further behind. In the end, he came in third.

He landed, took off his goggles and climbed out of the cockpit. The winning pilot was already standing by his plane. Roscoe caught up to him and said, "You flew a great race. I couldn't keep ahead of you."

"Roscoe, I've long admired your flying skills. I'm honored to have beaten you this time. I'm sure you will be a fierce competitor for the next race."

Roscoe turned back to his plane where Gilmore was waiting. He climbed into the cockpit and looked at

Gilmore. "You know, boy, I think your weight may be causing the problem. Between you and me, we are too heavy to race together. I'm afraid it's time for you to retire from racing."

He taxied to the hangar and turned off the engine. When the propeller stopped, they climbed out and made their way to Roscoe's car for the ride home.

"You know Gilmore, in the nine months we've flown together, you've logged twenty-five-thousand miles in the air. I'd say that's history making. Don't worry though, we can still fly together, just not in races. You'll do fine for air-shows and exhibitions, and of course you can still tag-along when I go golfing." He chuckled. Having Gilmore on the course was an advantage for Roscoe's group. They never had to wait long to play the next hole. The golfers ahead of them rushed to finish their putts so that they could have plenty of space between them and the big lion.

When Gilmore reached his full height and weight as an adult lion, Roscoe knew he had to give up his flying companion for good. For a while he had Gilmore's cage at the Burbank Airport, but eventually he arranged for Gilmore to live at Goebel Lion Farm where he was born.

Roscoe tried to visit Gilmore when he could, but once had to go eight years without seeing him. By the time he finally got a chance to visit him, Gilmore had

ROSCOE AND GILMORE HUGGING.

grown to 600 pounds! The keeper of the jungle park warned Roscoe to approach Gilmore carefully since it had been so long since he'd seen him.

"That lion will know me," Roscoe assured him, reaching his hand through the cage right up to Gilmore's mouth. "Hi, my old co-pilot. You know me, don't you."

The keeper's mouth hung open as the full-grown beast leaned out of his cage and docilely licked his former master's hand.

"I didn't believe it possible," the keeper said. "I've heard of lions remembering their masters a year or even two years, but eight years—"

"Gilmore, will always be my buddy."

Interesting Facts About
Roscoe Turner and Gilmore

1. Roscoe was born September 29, 1895. Cars were very new at that time. Most people traveled by horse and buggy, bicycles or trains.

2. Roscoe was the oldest of eight children. It was common to have large families in those days to help maintain the home and farm. His brother, Abe, who was closest to him in age, fulfilled their father's dream of having a banker in the family.

3. When Roscoe was a boy, many children, especially in the farming communities attended a one-room schoolhouse. This meant there was only one teacher for grades 1 through 10. There were no educational standards in Mississippi when Roscoe attended school. If your teacher decided you were finished with school, then you graduated.

4. His favorite subjects in school were Geography, Arithmetic, and History. He didn't like English very much. He couldn't remember how to use plurals and tense. In later years he learned how to correct that.

5. Hot air balloons were the first forms of human flight. They were used during battles to spy on the enemies. The very first passengers were not human, but animals: a duck a rooster, and a sheep named Montauciel, which in English means climb to the sky. They landed safely after their flight and told everyone about their adventure with baa's, quacks, and cock-a-doodle-doos.

6. During his years in Memphis, Roscoe had many jobs besides shipping clerk, ice truck driver, and mechanic's assistant. He chauffeured for Aunt Mollie's boarding house, and for the wealthy banker Mr. Frank F. Hill and his wife. In Mr. Hill's garage he learned a lot about Cadillacs and Packards, that were new brands of cars at the time. Then a Packard truck dealer, Jerome P. Parker-Harris Company, hired him as a salesman and mechanic.

7. The Great War, the War to End all Wars, the War of the Nations, were all different names for World War 1 which the United States entered on April 6, 1917.

8. While barnstorming, when Roscoe wanted to land his plane, he'd look at the cows. He learned they were nature's weather vane and usually turned their tails to the wind.

9. His favorite color was blue which is why he designed and wore a robin's-egg blue colored uniform.

10. Roscoe was married twice, but never had children.

11. Roscoe was always nervous when giving speeches in front of large crowds. He felt insecure because he had so little formal education. It was his single biggest regret.

12. For good luck before races, Roscoe flew with a rabbit's foot, a live turtle, and a small teddy bear.

13. Once when Roscoe was driving in a rainstorm with Gilmore sitting in the passenger seat, he skidded into another car. The frightened lion leaped out of the car. People walking on the sidewalks screamed running to their houses for safety. They thought a wild lion was on the loose!

14. The Humane Society demanded Gilmore have a parachute, so Roscoe outfitted him with his very own. Then as he grew, larger ones were made.

15. On radio programs for children, Roscoe tapped into the kids sense of adventure to excite them about airplanes. He supported many youth organizations including the Boy Scouts.

16. After he hung up his racing wings in 1939, he operated a flying school during World War II and trained over 3,300 men to be pilots.

17. After Gilmore retired completely and wasn't with Roscoe, people often asked why he still paid his food bills. He answered that for many years, Gilmore had paid his bills and that now it was his turn.

18. He predicted that in the future everyone would have a small airplane. He even envisioned them having flying automobiles so that when they went to buy a car, the salesman would ask them if they wanted it with or without wings.

19. President Richard M. Nixon invited Roscoe and his wife to an honorary dinner on August 13, 1969, for the Apollo 11 astronauts. Michael Collins, one of the three astronauts on the first moon-landing mission the previous month, was invited over to the table where Roscoe and the President were seated. Years later, Collins became director of the National Air & Space Museum and after Roscoe died, wrote

a letter to his wife. He wrote that Roscoe had been the graduation speaker when he received his wings and continued that it was the best speech he had ever heard.

20. Many of those who came into contact with Roscoe, former flight students, visitors, those who listened to his speeches, told him it was because of him that they became interested in aviation. It was then he realized that all the times he had taken risks testing the limits of airplanes and designing new ones, to keep aviation in the forefront of the public's mind, that it was worthwhile. This was his legacy and he was proud of it.

Roscoe Turner standing on a Navy airplane wing.

Roscoe Turner's Major Awards

1. Roscoe was the only pilot to win the Thompson Trophy three times.

2. He won the Bendix, the Harmon and the Henderson Trophies.

3. He set many coast-to-coast flying records.

4. He set new transcontinental record from New York to Los Angeles.

5. In 1933 and 1938, he received the Cliff Henderson Trophy as America's No.1 speed flier.

6. He set a record from Mexico City to Los Angeles carrying eleven passengers.

7. In 1952, through an Act of Congress, he was awarded the Distinguished Flying Cross from the United States Air Force.

8. He received the American Legion Distinguished Citizens Award in 1969.

9. He received the Distinguished National Veterans Award in 1969.

10. In 1975, he was inducted into the National Aviation Hall of Fame.

Acknowledgements

Several years ago, during my first trip to the National Air and Space Museum, Udvar-Hazy Center in Chantilly, Virginia, I noticed the captivating display of Roscoe Turner and his pet lion, Gilmore. Seeing it caused the spark that began this story. I am indebted to my husband Larry for taking me to that exhibit and for not complaining too often about me spending time with another man, Roscoe Turner.

In researching this book, I traveled to the Indianapolis Historical Museum to read Roscoe Turner's journal, numerous original newspaper clippings and magazine articles stored there. Nicole Poletika, Collections Assistant in the Reference Department, pulled newspaper clippings and information that were instrumental in kick-starting my research. I am grateful to her for a job well done. I could not have completed this project without the assistance of John Waggener, archivist for the American Heritage Center, University of Wyoming, who gathered digital photos from their extensive collection of Roscoe Turner. Also, Piper Thompson, A/V archives assistant who sent digital photos to my book designer. Thank you.

I gleaned many facts from Carroll V. Glines book, *Roscoe Turner Aviation's Master Showman*, which is a part of the Smithsonian History of Aviation Series. Without his work, it would have taken me much longer to research Roscoe Turner's life.

Many thanks to my brother, Lynwood, who has flown everything from fixed-wing to glider airplanes. He helped me write the flying lesson scene, making it more accurate than I ever could.

I want to express my appreciation to Robert Novell for reading my Author's Note and giving suggestions to make the aviation history part of my manuscript better. He was a corporate pilot also known as "freight dog", who began his flying career in 1979 and finally hung up his wings January 1, 2010. His input was invaluable.

I appreciate the efforts of my first editor, Laurie Rosin, who started me off in the right direction with her detailed editing years ago when I began this journey. Then to my present editor, Tammy Hensel, (no known relation), who made my story better than I ever imagined it could be. Her edits and suggestions were spot on. How she maintained her patience during some of my revisions I'll never know. I am most grateful to both her infinite patience and expertise.

Thank you to Liz Mertz for her complete editing of my final draft.

To my book designer of many years, Jill Ronsley, thank you for making my book look and read its' best.

And to my goofy dog, Sandi, who gave me comical relief when words wouldn't come to mind.

This project has taken what seems a lifetime to write, and during the course of it I may have forgotten someone who helped me accomplish my goal of getting Roscoe's story told. If I have failed to mention you, I apologize, it was not my intention.

Sources

Burgan, Michael and Robert Brown. *John Glenn: Young Astronaut*. Childhood of Famous Americans Series. Aladdin Paperbacks. September 1, 2000.

CBC Kids. "4 fun facts about hot air balloons". www.cbc.ca/kidscbc2/the-feed/4-fun-facts-about-hot-air-balloons.

Davies, Ronad Edward George. *Airlines of the United States Since 1914*. London: Putnam, 1972.

Ducksters Education Site. "Aircraft and WWI." https://www.ducksters.com/history/world_war_i/aviation_and_aircraft_of_ww1.php.

Fannon-Langston, Diane. "Time Machine: Co. Roscoe Turner, Legendary Speed Pilot Christened Air Service in Cedar Rapids." *The Gazette*, Grand City, Iowa, May 13, 1917. In Archives Roscoe Turner, 1932.

145

Glenn, Jr., John. *John Glenn: A Memoir*. Doubleday Dell. 1999.

Glines, C.V.. "A Showman Takes The Lead." *Aviation History Magazine*. January 29, 2018. Article number 508.

Glines, Carroll V. *Roscoe Turner, Aviations Master Showman*. Washington and London: Smithsonian Institution Press. 1995.

O'Neil, Paul. *Barnstormers and Speed Kings*. Alexandria, VA.: Time-Life Books. 1981.

Onkst. David H. "Roscoe Turner." Centennial of Flight. www.centennialofflight.net/essay/Explorers_Record_Setters_and_Daredevils/turner/EX22.htm

Swain, Gwenyth. *World War I: An Interactive History Adventure*. Putnam. February 1, 2012.

History for Kids. "World War I." www.historyforkids.nct/world-war-one.html

About the Author

As a child, Boots Hensel enjoyed going to airshows at nearby military bases with her family. At that time she had no idea she would grow up to be an award-winning author of children's books. A display about the life of Roscoe Turner at the National Air and Space Museum, Udvar-Hazy Center in Chantilly, Virginia, reminded her of the thrill she experienced in those days, igniting a desire to present his story to young readers.

Boots travels to speak at zoos, libraries, and schools. She is a member of Tallahassee Writers Association, Society of Children's Book Writers and Illustrators, Florida Authors and Publishers Association and Panama City Writers Association. She participates in local children's literacy functions through the Rotary Read Aloud Program.

Boots lives in Florida with her college sweetheart and husband of 53 years, Larry, and their dog, Sandi.

You can learn more about Boots and her books: *The Zoopendous Surprise* (Pleasant Street Press, 2009) and award-winning *Johari's Joy* (Kimber Court Press, 2013), both in their second printings, on her website www.bootshensel.com.

CPSIA information can be obtained
at www.ICGtesting.com
Printed in the USA
JSHW012341140920
7907JS00003B/141